Book I of The Immortal Epic

IMMORTAL JOURNEY

BY
KEVIN D. BLACKMON

ASCENDANT PUBLISHING
NORTH CAROLINA
2010

Published by Ascendant Publishing

Copyright © 2008 by Kevin D. Blackmon

Cover art by Darryl Taylor
Copyright © 2008 by Kevin D. Blackmon

ISBN-13: 978-0-9844721-0-9

Printed in the United States of America

IMMORTAL
JOURNEY

PROLOGUE

Wood blinds were closed to the afternoon sun reflecting off the Mediterranean Ocean. Tall terracotta pots, blooming with an array of color, lined the terrace like every other villa that dotted the hillside. A light breeze spread the soft fragrance of flowers to add to the calming atmosphere that is Italy.

Inside this particular villa was a different atmosphere all together. Inside, you felt as if you had been transported to the operating room of a space station. Where you would expect to see antique wood furniture, you saw smoked glass tables and brushed aluminum chairs. Where you would expect to see a simple iron stove, you saw reflective counter tops. The walls were stark white with an opaque black trim, and the floor was composed of black marble tiles. The house was spotless.

I stepped out of the washroom. I was barefoot, wearing boot cut jeans and a plain white shirt. With my shaved head and face, I looked flawlessly clean. I walked into the dining room and took a seat at the table. The atomic clock on the wall showed that it was currently 06:59.37 P.M. As soon as I read it, the wonderful buzz from the exhaust of a Porsche Cayman S drew near and brought a smile to my face. I heard the car come to a stop and the engine shut off. I focused my hearing. I heard her sigh heavily.

"Do you love him?" she asked.

Her warm, soothing voice normally brought calmness over me, but with this particular question that escaped her lips, I found myself holding my breath, waiting for an answer.

"Because you know why he has come." She didn't answer the question.

My heartbeat quickened as I listened for her feelings. She was the only one in the car. She was the only one that asked and had the power to answer in her world between the doors of her German sports car.

"But I'm not yet sure if I can accept it," she said.

I remained motionless as I continued to focus my hearing. I heard the car door open and her sandals touch the stone drive. The door was shut, and her footsteps were heard approaching her Italian getaway. I stood, straightened my shirt, and walked toward the door. The biometric lock approved her thumb print, and she walked in.

"Kevin," she said, throwing her arms around me.

I closed my eyes and succumbed to her embrace. I managed to say her name, "Seraphine," as I breathed in the hypnotic combination of her perfume, shampoo, and body lotion. I wasn't sure how I had survived the past month without her in my arms.

After a long moment, we pulled away slowly. I took her hand and led her into the dining room. I pulled a chair out for her, and she thanked me.

"So how was Tokyo?" I asked, glad to see her home.

"Oh, it was awesome as always," she answered with a big smile and a sparkle in her eyes as she remembered the tech shows that she attended.

I poured her a glass of ice water and brought it to her.

"Thank you," she told me, as she is always courteous. "So how have you been?" she asked. "Have I missed any excitement?"

"I've been okay," I answered with a little nod, "but I must say that it's been quite lonely without you," I teased as I sat at the round, smoked glass table next to her.

A warm, blushing smile spread across her face. "Aww, you are so very sweet. I may have stayed busy on my trip, but you were always on my mind."

I returned a warm smile of my own and laid a hand on hers. I saw my silhouette in her green eyes, and it triggered the memory of the day we met.

It was February of 2006. I was in D.C. with the owner of the coffee shop that I managed. I could always bring a laugh from the customers when I told them I didn't drink coffee, and I didn't tell the owner until after I had the job. Knowing that he knew I didn't like coffee, you can imagine my amusement when he asked if I would like to attend a coffee convention in D.C. with him. He told me that after the convention, we could take in some of the sites so I went.

Bitterly cold, that was my first thought when we arrived at the U.S. capital. Even through my thick leather coat, the wind cut like a knife. We dropped our bags off at the hotel room and walked across the street to the convention center.

Inside, it still wasn't that warm. Because of the high ceilings, all the heat was well above us, but at least we were out of the wind. It took me a while of walking among the coffee drinkers before the chill subsided.

Overall, the convention was pretty boring with vendors trying to talk us into thinking that we couldn't have a successful coffee shop without their product. There was a latte art competition that kept my attention for quite some time. It was interesting to see people draw a wreath with milk froth and be graded on it.

After a few hours of examining the print quality of custom labels for coffee bean bags and comparing the thickness of plastic cups, we couldn't take it any longer. We walked outside to find that, even though it was still cloudy, it was no longer windy, and it had actually warmed up a little.

We walked through the National Gallery of Art to get to the National Museum of Natural History where the Hope Diamond was on display. The 45.5 carat stone, which is believed to be cursed to anyone who makes claim to it, was on a pedestal in a room on the second floor. It was set on a slow spin within a glass box. I spent a few minutes looking at the diamond and reading the story posted on the wall before leaving the crowded room to look at dinosaur skeletons.

As I walked along the banister heading for the stairs, I heard a woman's voice say "*Hi,*" but it seemed to come from within my head. I stopped, and my eyes quickly targeted an unbelievably beautiful young woman on the ground level looking up at me from the path of the huge African elephant that greets the museum attendees. Reading my lips as I returned the "Hi," she smiled at me.

I made my way down where she met me at the foot of the stairs. As my boss was off looking at fossils from the Cretaceous period, as I had planned to do, I was instead sidetracked with a 5'8" brunette who pulled me into the shadows behind one of the many columns. Without a word, she took my hands and placed them under her long, straight hair to her ears. I was a bit confused at first but quickly felt the finely crafted ears that were trademarked by the elves.

My excitement could clearly be seen on my face, but I held my questions because I feared one of the many visitors would overhear, so I played her game. I took her thumbs and, as I extended my canines, placed them to the tips. I saw a gasp flash across her face as I felt her skin break and "vampire" silently form from her lips.

I tasted her blood as she pulled her hands away from my mouth to examine the small wounds. She licked the remaining bit of blood from her thumbs before digging into her small designer purse to reveal an ink pen. She took my left hand and wrote in the palm. She added a kiss and closed my fingers over it. "I've given you my name," she said to me in a warm, beautiful tone. "May I have yours?"

She held my hand between hers, and I could see my silhouette in her eyes. "I'm Kevin."

"Well, Kevin," she said with a smile, "it is very nice to meet you, and I'm sure we will see each other again."

She dropped the pen in her purse while she kept hold of my hand. She stepped out of the shadow that we occupied, holding on as long as possible before letting go. I watched her walk away in her boot cut jeans and thick, black turtleneck. Just before stepping into the foyer of the museum, she looked back to give me another wonderful smile. Once she was out of sight, I looked at my palm to see her name, "Seraphine." Her number followed with a smiley face.

"Kevin?" her voice brought my thoughts to the present as I saw myself again in her eyes.

"Yes, I'm here," I told her with a smile, shaking off my memories. "I was just remembering the day we met."

She broke into laughter. "You were so nervous."

"I can't believe you would say that!" I exclaimed, playfully shocked. "I believe I was keeping my cool," I continued, noticeably holding back a laugh.

"Oh, you were nervous," she stressed. "You could barely utter your own name."

We both laughed because she had me with that.

"I had tried to keep my cool, but I guess that kept me too tight to speak."

"Too tight to speak?" she laughed out at me. "I held your hand because I was afraid you were about to pass out."

"Well, I'm glad you held me up," I said sarcastically.

"Oh, I've missed you." Her laughter subsided, and her wonderful smile warmed the room. "I could definitely get used to coming home to you."

Now that made me blush. "You make me feel so special, and that's why I've come," I told her with a loving smile.

Seraphine remained quiet as she listened to my every word. Her keen instincts told her why I had come.

"From the moment I met you at the museum, I felt that you were the one. I wanted to get to know you. I needed to know, not only in my heart but in my mind, that you deserve immortality." I paused for a moment as I took in the beauty that sat before me. Her emerald eyes seemed all the more glorious against her lightly tan skin and brown hair.

"Would you like to share eternity with me," I asked her, "to pass through the ages unchanged, untouched by sickness and impervious to decay? Before you answer that, I would like to tell you about the night I was forever changed, about the night I met a vampire."

CHAPTER I

KEVIN OF SEAGROVE

It was 3:05 A.M. Sunday, July 14, 1996. I was 18 years old and living in the small town of Seagrove, North Carolina with my mom and step-dad. I had a third shift job at a plastic manufacturing company, but I was off work that night. My job was boring, but I was saving my money to move to Myrtle Beach, South Carolina with my drummer. We were planning to move down in spring of the following year and get our music career going.

We named our band Visionary, and we had been together for a little over a year. We had written a few songs that we played at parties, but we hadn't been in a studio to record anything; we hadn't found the right singer for our style of music. With country being the music of choice in the area, it was hard to find someone that actually liked heavy metal, much less sing it.

We always practiced at my drummer's apartment because it was easier for me to carry my guitar and amplifier there than it was for him to carry his drum set to my house. We usually started about 6:30 in the evening and played until 10:00 that night. Because of his neighbors living so close, we couldn't play any later, or they would call the cops on us.

I remember the first time a cop showed up at the door. He said, "It sounds good, fellas, but your neighbors are complaining. I'm gonna have to ask you to turn it down."

We thought it was cool that, of all the cops in hick town, we got the one that liked heavy metal. Since then, we tried to keep an eye on the time, but whenever our friends from another band came over to practice with us, the music would be interrupted by a heavy knock on the door at 10:01.

We practiced the previous night, but we were finished well before our curfew. We ordered a few pizzas, and the guys from both bands hung out to watch the Moronathon on TV. Oh, it was hilarious. We laughed so hard, we cried.

I was normally driving home as the sun peeked over the horizon, but I got in early that morning. I quietly carried my gear upstairs to my room. My brother's bedroom was across the hall, but our dad had custody of him that weekend.

Neill is six years younger than me. Because he wasn't of legal age to make decisions for himself, the judge gave our dad custody of him. The judge's thinking was, since I chose to stay with mom, Neill should stay with dad to make it an even split.

So without my brother there to wake up, I began playing my electric guitar with only an artificial jack-o'-lantern lighting my room. I was sitting Indian-style on the carpeted floor as I worked out a new song riff. It was awesome. It was one of the coolest rhythms that I had ever heard, and I was its creator. Without losing the tempo, I stood. I turned away from the light to see my lanky shadow divide the room and break the wall. My black Jackson Kelly guitar hung low, making me look like an axe murderer who had just claimed another head. I felt the rhythm pulsing within me. I closed my eyes and gave myself to the music. I played the arrangement of chords over and over. My heart was beating with the rhythm. I swayed along as if in a trance.

A cool breeze alerted me, and I turned to see someone sitting inside the room on the window sill. My blue curtains flowing with the wind made it look like a ghost, or maybe it was my overactive imagination playing a trick on me. My body froze as my brain tried to process the information that my eyes were gathering. Was this my imagination? Could this be a ghost? Maybe he's a thief or a murderer! My brain sped up to quickly assess the situation so a course of action could be determined.

He smiled and clapped lightly. "Cool tune. You are getting good."

My guitar squeaked as I rushed for the light switch. In a flash, the room was illuminated, and I saw my intruder. My fears washed away with the shadows as my brain finally registered what he was, and I wished I were like him.

We stared at each other for a long moment as

the feedback from my guitar grew loud enough to draw my attention. Without taking my eyes away from him, I caught the volume knob of the guitar with my little finger to silence the hum.

The intruder slowly stepped away from the window to not seem threatening. Magically, the window slid shut behind him.

Amazed, I finally spoke. "You are an elf."

He sat on the edge of the bed and looked around at how I had decorated my bedroom. My room was big, with plenty of walking space. My bed was positioned along the far side of the left wall. I had an entertainment center opposite my bed. There were two windows: one on the far wall and one on the right, which was the front of the house. I had a guitar stand below the front window. My Crate Blue Voodoo amplifier was kept behind the door. I had posters pinned to the ceiling in a circular formation as if they were radiating from the light of my chandelier, posters ranging from Megadeth and Joe Satriani to Jenny McCarthy and The X-Files. I didn't have any posters covering my floral wallpaper. I wanted my room to have the right balance of cool and beautiful which I was always working on.

The stranger studying my room was the same height and build as me. Our hair was the same length, but his was strawberry blond where mine was golden blond. He was wearing a plain black shirt with jeans and sandals. He could almost fit in as human except for his finely crafted elvish features. Yes, the ears gave him away.

"My name is Kieran," he finally said to me, "and I am an elven vampire."

"Why are you here? Am I to be your next meal?" I asked jokingly. I've always been one to crack jokes in serious situations; it helps me stay calm.

Kieran laughed out a "no."

Now that his laugh had lightened the mood a bit, I asked him a more serious question. "So are you good or evil?"

He smiled at me for asking such an honest, straightforward question. "Everyone does what they believe to be right to get what they want," he explained to me. "So in a way, there is no such thing as evil."

I turned off my amplifier, unplugged my guitar and sat it on its floor stand. I did all that with barely a glance away from Kieran. I walked slowly toward him to examine him closer. "So how old are you, and where are you from?"

"I was born in the elven city of Sungrove in the year 262 AD, by your calendar, so that makes me 1,734 years old. Sungrove existed in Romania. It was destroyed the same night that I became a vampire in 449."

I was noticeably amazed by his answer. "I'm 18," I told him with a laugh because I was so young in comparison.

"Yes, I am very old," he said with a smile.

"Do you kill people and drink their blood?" I asked curiously.

"Yes, we drink blood and avoid sunlight, but we don't kill people," he explained. "We are not the creatures that you see in the movies. Well, my race of vampires isn't," he corrected himself.

I was starting to feel okay about a stranger being in my room, even if that stranger happened to be a vampire. It wasn't like I could do anything about it if he wanted to drink my blood, right?

Because I didn't have chairs in my room, I sat Indian-style on the floor. "What is it with blood?" I asked him. "Why do vampires have to drink it?"

Kieran moved from the bed to the floor, so he didn't have to talk down to me. He also sat Indian-style, but he had his back against the bed. "Our strength and regenerative power burns a lot of energy. We can't digest food, so we must steal the energy from others to survive, or we will begin to decompose."

I grew up on a healthy diet of horror movies, so it was interesting to learn the science behind vampires. "How long can you go without blood before you notice signs of decomposition?" I asked him.

"I feel a difference after one day of not feeding," he answered me, "but I can make it quite a while before my body noticeably begins breaking down."

Kieran waited patiently for me to think how to word my next question. "So is it difficult, mentally, to feed on the living?" I finally asked him. I thought that, if a vampire hasn't come to me for a drink, then he must have come to turn me.

"No, it's not as hard as you would think," Kieran answered with a smile.

Now for what I believed was the most important question. "What about God?" I asked proudly. "What will He do with you if you somehow die after being a vampire? Will He send you to Hell?" If this vampire really was here to offer me immortality, I thought it would be a good idea to know all the ins and outs before I was tricked into letting him drain my soul away.

Kieran sighed heavily. He was quiet for a long moment, staring at the thick brown carpet as if lost in the past. It seemed he came fearing I would ask this question but hoped I wouldn't.

I had been attending a Southern Baptist church for more than nine years. I had been saved. I had been baptized. I may play heavy metal music, but I am definitely not an angry person. I'm like a superhero without the spandex, a monk without the robes. I stop to move turtles out of the road. I say I'm sorry when I have to kill a fly. I do my best to always tell the truth. I am constantly reaching for my view of personal perfection so that I can be a shining example of goodness in the universe. I doubted he could sway my faith, but I kept an open mind and waited patiently for what he had to say.

He straightened his legs and crossed his feet to relax a bit before answering. "One of the first signs of an intelligent race is the belief in a higher power. We look at ourselves and the world around us and ask 'how?' and 'why?'"

"I believe in evolution," I told him, "but even that has a beginning. Someone had to create space and matter for the Big Bang to happen."

"You're looking at it the wrong way, my young friend," he told me with a smile. "If what you are saying is true then who made God? Humans are still too young a race to comprehend the vastness of reality. Perhaps we all are," he added in a low tone, more to himself than to me. "We try to explain our existence with what we think is the obvious truth, and by doing so, we cloud our minds from what is real. What we believe to be real becomes our reality."

I stared blankly at the floor as I processed his every word.

"With your religion, Christianity," he continued, "God is a perfect being. What you have failed to see is that, for a being to be perfect, all their creations must be perfect. Perfection can only beget perfection. If God is the creator of all things, He cannot be perfect because His creations are not perfect. If one part of the equation is wrong then the answer will not be as you expected."

"But God gave us free will," I spoke up, proud of my answer. "We were created perfect, but with free will, we are able to stray."

"But with limitless knowledge, God would know everything that everyone will do and have that factored into His master plan," he fired back effortlessly. "So there is no such thing as free will," he said with a smile, shaking his head.

My brain worked for something else to say but came up with nothing.

"Now here's something for you to think about," he said, holding up a finger. "If God is all powerful, how could He create Satan, knowing that he will be bad, and then allow him to continue opposing Him?"

"I don't know," I admitted. I waited for the answer, but he didn't give it, only a winning smile. "So if you don't believe in God, what do you think happens when we die?" I asked. "Do you believe we just cease to exist?"

His expression turned sad as he looked down at his hands, which were together on his lap. "I once believed that, when we die, our spirit flies into the Sun to join our loved ones. After living nearly two millennia and witnessing cultures and religions from all over the world, I now struggle with my own."

There was silence between us for a moment. I enjoyed talking about religion with him, even if he did seem to win that battle. I needed to do some research, so maybe I could best him next time.

I finally asked, "Since you live forever, do you try to make friends, or do you avoid seeing them die by staying alone?"

Kieran lifted his eyes to meet mine. "Oh, do I have a story for you," he said through a hard smile.

ACT I

449 AD

CHAPTER II

SUNRISE

Blackness faded to light as the sun rose over the eastern mountains. There was a cool mist in the air and dew on the leaves. Birds perched in the trees signaled the dawn of a new day.

With my hands behind my head, I lay on the roof of my parent's house. The roof was angled, and I was facing the sun. I watched the sunrise every morning. Like all Wood Elves, I believed that the Sun began the cycle of life and will one day take it away. It contains the spirits of the dead. All creatures and beings which once lived on this green Earth now reside there. So while I smiled up at the sun, I felt that my ancestors were smiling down at me.

I heard the click of the door latch below and someone step outside.

"Kieran?" my sister called out for me. She

knew that I was lying on the rooftop, but she wondered if I were awake.

I took one last refreshing breath before starting my day. "Yes?"

"Come on, or we'll be late," she said as she closed the door behind her and speedily walked away.

I dropped from the rooftop and ran to catch up with her. "Good morning, Kel," I greeted her happily.

Without looking at me, she answered. "Good morning."

Kelena and I were twins. With our finely crafted features and green eyes, we made a beautiful pair. We even dressed the same, with brown breeches and a dark green tunic. The only real difference between us, besides gender of course, was our hair. We both had long, strawberry blond hair, but I kept my hair straight and tied back with a ribbon where hers had large curls.

At 5'7", we had grown to our full height, but we were still quite young. Because we were elves, we could grow exceptionally old. The average life span of an elf is around 800 years, but it isn't uncommon for one to grow as old as 1,000 years or beyond. Kelena and I were 187 years old. We had centuries of life ahead of us, but right now, we had to get to school.

We walked at a quickened pace through the elven city of Sungrove. The ground was covered with a soft carpet of moss that felt great beneath bare feet. Other elves and fairies were coming outside to start their day. I smiled and waved at everyone, but Kelena seemed focused on getting to class on time. She stared straight ahead with no expression on her face, no acknowledgment of her brother walking next to her.

I noticed beyond her an elderly couple sitting outside having breakfast. The man was motioning for me to come over. "Wait just a moment," I told Kelena.

She stopped to wait for me. The elderly woman smiled and waved at her. She returned a little smile and a short wave.

"Take these. We cannot eat all this," the elderly man told me as he handed me a couple of green apples.

I gladly took the apples. "Much thanks to you," I said with a smile and a nod before returning to Kelena's side.

"Have a wonderful day, young ones," the elderly woman said to us.

"And a wonderful day to you, to you both," I told them. I handed my sister an apple as I started to eat mine, and we continued to school.

We passed house after house. I sensed from the moment she called for me that something was troubling her but believed she would have told me by now. I allowed her more time to open up to me as I finished my apple. I ate it all the way to the stem, spitting out the seeds of course. At that moment, I saw a fairy flying by, so I thumped the stem at him.

"OUCH!" the fairy yelled, but he was more startled than hurt. "Oh, hi Kieran," he greeted with a wave and a smile as he continued on his way.

I tried to hold back my laughter as I returned the greeting, "Hi Fez."

As Kelena and I continued our walk, I looked to her and saw that she was deep in thought. I took her hand in mine, and by touching her, I created a psychic link. She didn't object and allowed me to catch glimpses of her thoughts. In my mind, I saw flashes of her leading us out of Sungrove and over the mountains to the forests that lay beyond. She was tired of waking up in the same city every day, tired of seeing the same people, tired of living the same life. She was tired of repeating the same day over and over.

I released her hand, severing the psychic link. We stopped walking, and she looked at me. "Will you come with me if I leave?"

I kissed her on the forehead, which is the custom for elf families, before answering her. "Of course; I cannot live without you."

Kelena took my hand, and with a telepathic message, she said, *"And I cannot live without you. You are my brother and my friend."* We shared a loving embrace before continuing to class.

We walked hand in hand until we reached Yuri's house, which was in the center of the city. Every morning, he taught minor spells to the young elves of Sungrove. He was also Sungrove's guardian. Yuri may have stayed in the form of a very young elf, but he was actually a Yellow Dragon.

There were four elf cities: Ashwood, Lylandria, Magestice, and Sungrove. Sungrove was the smallest of the four. Each city was protected by at least one dragon because the dragons believed that one day, when the elven race was large enough, we should inherit the Earth. The dragons barely concerned themselves with the lesser races. The centaurs, goblins, satyrs, dwarves, and humans were always fighting over territories, but the dragons would not tolerate any attack made against the elves. We are a loving race that maintains balance and harmony with nature.

Yuri may have been among the youngest of the

dragons, and he may have appeared to be an elf under the age of 100, but looks can be deceiving. A dragon of any age, especially a Yellow Dragon, was a powerful creature.

The other students were already seated and ready for the day's lesson. They were all outside Yuri's home in chairs constructed of living vines arranged in a semicircle around Yuri. The students were talking amongst themselves as they waited for the last two students.

Yuri stood to greet us. "My beautiful pupils, Kieran and Kelena." He welcomed us both with a hug as he did every morning.

It didn't matter how many times I saw him, his gold, reptilian eyes always caught my attention. His blond hair was tied back into a ponytail, and his nails were long but kept neat.

Gesturing with his right hand, he said, "Please, have a seat," and two vines sprouted from the ground to form chairs.

Kel and I took our seats among the other seven students. She sat between me and her boyfriend, Trevor. She cut him a cute smile.

With a smile of his own, Trevor said, "It's about time you show up. Yuri was about to start without you."

Kelena didn't try explaining her tardiness. She and the other students were ready for class and were respectful to the teacher.

Yuri was seated and again ready to teach today's lesson. "A glorious morning to you, pupils," he said to the entire class.

"A glorious morning to you," we, the students,

voiced in unison.

"Before I get into today's lesson, I would like everyone to show me what you learned yesterday."

Everyone put their hands together, palms up, to show the teacher that we had been keeping up with our lessons.

I had practiced all yesterday afternoon, so I knew exactly what to do. I blocked out my surroundings and stared intensely at my hands. Moisture from the air began gathering to form a puddle of water an inch above my hands. The water then began to form a tiny being, starting with the feet and moving up to form the legs. Within seconds, the pool of water transformed into a fairy. I touched its forehead to make a ripple run through it. When the ripple reached its limit, it began to freeze on the way back to where I touched it. I then let my ice fairy slowly spin above my hands and looked to my teacher to show that I was finished.

Yuri stood and walked over for a closer look at my work. "She is very beautiful, Kieran. Good work." He rubbed me on the head and gave me a smile before moving on to look at the other sculptures.

Kelena had not been paying attention to what I was creating. She had been busy with her own work. Now that Yuri had complimented me, she turned to see for herself. She was a little surprised at how perfect it turned out and recognized the fairy as it spun in my hands. "Hey, it's Tess. That is really good."

Kelena had made a weeping willow tree. I leaned forward to look past her to see that Trevor had made an oak tree. I looked at the other students' sculptures to see a bowl of fruit, a bouquet of daisies, a deer, a bust of Yuri, an eagle, and the sun.

After Yuri looked over all the ice sculptures, he returned to the center of the class. "Good work, students," he congratulated. "All of you did very well. Now for today's lesson, we are going to use magic to return our creations back to nature. Position your creation as if you are going to reverse the spell." Yuri created a miniature palace of ice in the palms of his hands to better demonstrate the new spell.

Everyone had their hands together with their palms up and their ice sculpture floating above them.

Yuri continued, "Spread your fingers out wide and imagine pulling the surrounding light into your hands. Once you see it forming in your mind, try to compact the light into a tiny ball. Feed more light into it so that it grows to surround the ice." As he was telling us how to cast the new spell, he himself was casting the spell on his ice palace.

Small spheres of light formed around the elves ice sculptures. Some of the elves were a little slower than others at getting their light to form.

"Once the light totally surrounds the ice," Yuri said, "make the light hot very quickly so that the melted ice does not drip onto your hands." Yuri's palace exploded into a flash of light as he watched his students concentrate on the spell.

I looked at my beautiful ice fairy. It was slowly spinning within the sphere of light. I touched the fairy's face with a finger. I didn't want to destroy it. I wanted to keep it forever. The sphere of light dissipated.

Yuri noticed that my light had gone out before melting away my sculpture. He walked over to help me with the spell. "What happened?" he asked. "Do you need some help?"

I looked up at him with my fairy still floating above my palms. "No, teacher, I'm sure I will have no trouble with the new spell. It's just that I don't want to destroy it."

Yuri smiled and asked, "How will you keep it? You know it will eventually melt away."

For a moment, I imagined the entire city melting away, and I was left in the forest alone. I looked back to my sculpture and nodded my head sadly. Without a word, I recast the light spell around it. The sphere of light grew so bright that the fairy within could not be seen. The light dimmed just as quickly and faded away to reveal my empty hands. My pretty fairy was gone without a trace. Not a single drop of water was left on my hands.

"Very good," Yuri said before returning to his chair.

I looked away from my hands and saw that the rest of the students had long since finished their spell casting and had been watching me. I straightened up in my chair and faced forward.

Yuri cleared his throat to get everyone's attention and continued with his lesson. "Cast your light spell again, and change the color of it. Make it your favorite color."

Everyone cast the spell again to create a sphere of light in the palm of their hand. The spheres began to shift colors throughout the spectrum. Mine was golden yellow like the sun. Kelena's was sky blue.

"Very good, pupils," Yuri complimented us. "Now let it fade away, and cast the spell again from the beginning. Create a sphere of ice. Cast a light spell to enclose it. Then, melt the ice away without letting it drip."

Smiling as all the students cast the spell perfectly, he said, "Excellent."

"Why doesn't it burn our hands?" Trevor asked.

Yuri answered, "You are the caster. While you have control of it, it cannot burn you, but if you release your heated sphere of light toward someone, it would become a fireball and burn them. Are there any more questions?" He waited a moment. "Then I will see everyone in the morning, and remember: Practice makes better. Perfect practice makes perfect. Be well, my friends."

When everyone stood, their chairs returned to the earth. Trevor took Kelena's hand. "Are you coming over later?"

"Of course," she said with a smile as Trevor kissed her tenderly on the nose, which is the custom for elf couples. Holding hands and eye contact as long as they could, they slowly walked in separate directions. Their fingers slid out of touch, and they waved to one another as they went to their homes for lunch.

As Kelena and I walked home, I practiced my new spell. At first, I cast the spell just as I did in class. I created a sphere of ice and quickly melted it away with a sphere of light. I then started throwing the spheres of ice into the air ahead of me and shooting them with fireballs. I laughed at the fun of it.

Kelena paid no attention as she still seemed lost in her thoughts of moving away from Sungrove. "I cannot wait to show mother and father our new spell," I told her as I continued to play.

Kelena snapped out of her daydream and looked at me with a smile. "I'll race you." At that moment, Kelena sprinted off.

I stopped my spell casting and ran. Through the city, we ran faster and faster. I got within arm's reach, but I could not pass her. She laughed because she knew she would win. She always won. Between the two of us, she was the faster one. Not to mention, she had a head start.

She reached home first and ran inside. I ran in right behind her. Our parents, Lily and Kip, were preparing the table for lunch.

"Look at the new spell that we learned today," Kelena said. She then looked at me, wanting me to show them.

With a smile, I created a small sphere of ice in my left hand and cast the new spell with my right to melt it away. The light then shifted through different colors before fading away.

"That is fantastic!" Lily exclaimed as she put her arms around us.

"Yes, that is great, children," Kip congratulated, walking around the table to hug us.

We all exchanged kisses on the forehead and sat down to eat. We were having salmon with red potatoes and white wine.

"Do you want to watch the sunset tonight?" Kelena asked me.

I answered with a nod because I had food in my mouth.

Kelena quickly finished her lunch, so she could

spend time with Trevor. She cleaned her dishes in a small tub of water and kissed our parents on the forehead before heading to the door. She looked back to me, "I won't be gone too long," she said, and she raced out.

"So when are you going to choose a mate?" my mother asked. "I'd like to see my grandchildren before I go to the Sun."

I paused between bites and pressed my lips together, staring quietly at my food.

"You will soon be finished with your Minor Magic courses," she continued. "Have you decided what you will do afterwards?"

I remained quiet. I had heard this countless times before.

"Your mother is right," Kip added. "You are 187 years old. Don't you think it's time to find someone and begin a family?"

I didn't finish my meal. I got up from the table, and just before raking my food into the trash, I thought to use the new spell to burn away the remaining food. I turned up my goblet of wine to drink the last couple of swallows before washing the glass.

I finally decided to answer their questions. "You know that I'm choosy when it comes to a mate. I would have chosen one already if I were not. I've been thinking about continuing my lessons at the Temple of High Magic."

"But that is in Magestice. You would have to move," Kip said, shocked that his son thought of moving away from his family.

I stood there, staring at the stone floor. I didn't make eye contact because I felt that I had hurt them with the suggestion of moving away.

"Have you told Kel of your plans?" my mother asked.

"No, but I am sure she will join me," I answered as I finally looked at her.

"You need to talk to her about it," Lily said, thinking that Kelena would never go along with it because she was so much in love with Trevor and could never leave him.

"Learning High Magic is a big commitment," Kip added. "It could take several hundred years."

"I will talk to Kel tonight and hear what she thinks," I told them as I walked over to Lily.

She looked up at me as I kissed her lightly on the forehead. "I don't want you to move away," she told me.

I took a deep breath. "I know, but I see no future for me here," I said sadly before moving to give Kip a kiss as well.

I stepped outside, and as I walked toward the mossy bank of the city stream, I untied the ribbon from my hair. I sat down to wash my hands and splash my face with water. As the ripples of the stream leveled out, I saw my sister become clear. Her green eyes stared back at me from the water's surface. I thought for a moment that she must see me as her reflection just as I see hers as mine.

SPLASH! I was unexpectedly splashed in the face with water. I looked up to see Tess, the fairy that I had sculpted earlier in class. She was laughing at me from across the stream. I jumped across the narrow creek and grabbed her before she could react, holding her close to me so she too would get wet.

"Stop!" she screamed. "You're getting me wet!"

I laughed and kissed her on the head. "My precious Tess, you know I love you," I said with a smile.

She screamed at me again. "Kieran, let me go! You're getting me all wet!" With another attempt to break free, I let her go. She then flew up and smacked me on the nose. She put her fists on her hips. "You got me wet," she said with a scowl.

I mocked her by putting my fists on my hips and repeating with the same scowl, "Well, you got me wet."

Her face lit up with a cute little smile, and she gave me a quick kiss on the nose. We stared at each other for a moment. Her black tunic swayed with the breeze. We had been best friends our entire lives. Her ebony hair was tied up in pigtails, and her sun kissed skin was flawless. To be only eight inches tall, she was as pretty as a sunrise.

I couldn't hold eye contact. I looked down at the moss beneath my feet. "Kel and I are going up on the mountain later to watch the sunset," I told her, to break the silence between us. Without raising my eyes to look back at her, I asked, "Would you like to join us?"

"I would, sweetie" she answered with a smile. She knew that between me and Kelena, I was the shy one and oh, how she loved to make me blush.

CHAPTER III

SUNSET

With Tess flying close by, my sister and I followed a narrow trail that led to the top of the nearest mountain. The forest was thick with very few beams of light reaching the ground. The sound of birds and locusts filled the warm afternoon air.

We reached an opening at the top of the mountain. We sat down to watch the sun fall behind the mountains that lay beyond. Tess sat on my shoulder and rested her head against my cheek. We sat quietly for several minutes, taking in nature's beauty, before I spoke. "Have you told Trevor that you want to leave Sungrove?" I asked Kelena without looking away from the wonderful view of the mountains.

"No. Not yet," she answered. "I don't know if he would want to leave."

"I told mother and father that after I complete

the Minor Magic courses, I want to attend the Temple of High Magic."

Kelena was noticeably excited. "That is a good idea. The Temple is in Magestice. That would be a great place to live."

At the same time, Tess was noticeably sad. She left my shoulder to look me straight in the face. "You're not going to leave me, are you?"

Her very words broke my heart. "No, I would not leave you. I want you to come with me."

Kelena followed with, "We love you, Tess. We would never leave you out of our lives."

The three of us watched the last remaining beams of light fade over the mountains. Kelena and I lay with our hands behind our heads and watched the stars appear. Tess lay on my stomach in the same position.

"So have you given much thought to the school of magic in which you will specialize?" Kelena asked me.

"Actually, I've given it a lot a thought," I answered her, "but I haven't yet decided. I hate to limit myself to one school, but one lifetime isn't enough to master them all. I had narrowed my choices down to either Conjuration or Illusion, but now I'm thinking more about Necromancy. Now, before you ask why I would want to raise the dead, let me explain. It's not that I want to breathe life into a corpse, but I believe, by understanding death, I will better understand life, and I can save all whom I love from dying."

I waited for Kelena to ask why I wouldn't want to join grandfather in the afterlife, but I heard nothing. Neither she nor Tess said a word. I raised my head to find Tess sound asleep on my stomach. I turned to look at Kel and saw that she too was asleep. I snickered and shook my head before turning my gaze back to the twinkling stars. It wasn't long before the peacefulness of the night made my eyelids too heavy to hold open, and I dozed off.

"Well, here we are. This is the spot," grandfather said to Kel and me as he led us out of the woods and to the edge of the mountain. The sun had just started to fall below the horizon. It was a beautiful sight.

I looked at Kel and saw that she was a kid again. She looked at me and asked, "What? What is it?" No doubt because I was staring at her.

"Come sit down," our grandfather told us. He was watching the sunset. Kel and I joined him, sitting on either side. "I come up here every evening," he said proudly without taking his eyes away from the horizon. He paused for a moment. His face grew sad, and he began to look every bit of 840 years old. "I come to wish your grandmother a goodnight," he continued.

I looked to the sun, curious of what he was speaking of.

"She is in the Sun," he explained as he must have read my thoughts. "All who have passed on fly into the Sun."

"How did grandmother die?" Kelena asked.

Grandfather put his arms around us. "It was her time to go. We are only on this earth for so long before the Sun calls us home."

"The Sun didn't want you to go with her?"

Kelena asked, trying to understand.

"My time will come. I had to stay here to help her make the journey." The look he saw on Kel's face told him that he should explain a bit more. "For a person to fly into the Sun, their body must be destroyed by fire. Your grandmother closed her eyes for the last time, so I had to send her home." He stared off, remembering that sad day. His eyes welled up with tears.

"Grandfather, why are you crying?" Kelena asked. "Shouldn't you be happy for her?"

He sniffled and wiped his face before turning a smile to Kelena. "I am, sweetheart. I am happy for her. It's just that I miss her very much. Delwen and I were married for 661 years, and there was rarely a day that we were apart."

"What would have happened if grandmother's body was never burned?" I asked.

"The body must be completely destroyed to release the spirit," he answered. His eyes now cleared from tears and filled with faith. "Her spirit would not be able to leave, and she would be bound to the Earth forever, never to reach the warm embrace of the Sun."

"Wouldn't the Sun burn everything up, grandfather?" I asked him.

"What?" he asked as he gave me a look like I should not be questioning the religion of the elves.

"Can't you smell the smoke?" I asked. "Can't you smell the smoke?"

I awakened to the faint smell of smoke. I cast the light spell and remembered where I was. I was on the mountain peak with Kel and Tess. "I smell smoke. Wake up! I smell smoke!"

Tess and Kelena were startled from their slumber. Tess flew up from my chest so I could stand.

"We have to get back!" I exclaimed.

Kelena and I ran down the trail toward Sungrove. Tess flew right behind us. We ran out of the forest and into the city to find that it was gone. The entire city had been destroyed. Only a few remains were left burning.

"Everything is gone!" Kelena screamed.

"Where is everyone? What has happened?" I asked aloud. I turned to Kelena to see that she was casting a spell, so I didn't interrupt her. She called rain clouds to put out the remaining fires.

"Over here! I've found something," Tess yelled out to us as our hair began to get wet from the rain.

We ran over to see that she had found hoof prints that led into the forest. "We should follow these before the rain washes them away," Kelena said.

At the edge of the forest, the three of us looked back at what used to be the elven city of Sungrove. Now it was a smoldering ruin of what was once our home.

Kelena started to cry as we turned away from the city and entered the dark forest. "Who would do this? Who would destroy our home?" she asked, all choked up. She sat on a rock at the edge of the trail.

I squatted down in front of her as Tess tried to comfort her by caressing her face and pushing the hair away from her crying eyes. "I don't know, Kel. I don't know," I finally answered sadly. I sat on the rock beside her and put a comforting arm around her.

Tess kissed her on the forehead. Tess then looked at me with the saddest of faces. My lips quivered at the sight of her upset, and she kissed them. She hugged my cheek and started to cry. She then kissed my nose, and we sat together for a few more moments.

I stood and offered a hand to Kel. "We need to go. We may lose them if we don't keep going," I told her. We wiped our eyes and continued.

We followed the trail for nearly an hour with hardly a word between us. The dark forest was eerily quiet. The only thing heard was the creaking of trees swaying in the night air, no owls, no frogs, nothing.

Suddenly, two werewolves leaped out from the dark! The night was now filled with bloodthirsty howls as we were attacked. One of the huge beasts backhanded me into a tree. The other knocked Kelena unconscious to the ground. It then jumped at Tess, but she blinded it with a flash of light and flew out of its way at the last second. The werewolf shook its head and regained its vision before leaping at her again. It swatted her down. As she tried to fly up out of the werewolf's reach, it caught her in its mouth. It ate her!

The werewolf that ate Tess bit the still unconscious Kelena on the back of the neck and picked her up. It carried her off into the darkness.

The other sank its teeth into my shoulder and threw me into the air. It then grabbed me again and shook me wildly before throwing me to the ground. The werewolf licked my wounds and looked at me with bloodthirsty eyes. Before the beast tore me apart, something ran into it, knocking it away from me. The werewolf turned its focus to the stranger. Before the cloaked warrior could react, the werewolf knocked him into a tree. The werewolf charged at blinding speed toward him, but the warrior leaped straight up into the trees. The werewolf slid to a stop and looked up. It walked around on all fours as it tried to catch his scent above. It could hear him leaping from tree to tree. Then there was silence.

The werewolf sniffed the air and pinpointed where he was. It leaped into the trees after him. The still cloaked warrior jumped to another tree before the werewolf got to him. They stood on large tree limbs, staring at one another. The mysterious warrior ripped his cloak away. He was actually a she, and she was a beautiful elf. She snapped her fists out to both sides, taking a fighting stance, and ghostly 10" blades appeared from each fist.

The werewolf growled and lunged toward her with snarling fury. She sidestepped the attack and sliced off one of its claws. As the werewolf tried to keep itself from falling, it grabbed her leg with its remaining hand and pulled her from the tree limb. They fell through the limbs to the ground. The elf warrior hit hard, and her weapons disappeared. The werewolf landed on its feet. She rolled over to see the werewolf lunging for her. Just before it sank its teeth into her face, she threw out an open palm to stop it with an invisible force. She threw the beast back. The werewolf's claws raked across the ground as it tried to stop from being pushed.

The beast charged toward her again. She pulled a dagger from a sheath strapped to the inside of her leg. She thrust the dagger in the side of the werewolf's neck. It grabbed her and threw her into a tree. The bloodthirsty monster slowly collapsed to the ground and transformed into an elf just before taking its last breath.

The mysterious female rushed over to check on me. She gasped at the sight of me but saw that I was still alive. She took me in her arms and ran. She carried me as if I weighed nothing through the dark forest and over the mountains. She was so fast. I slipped in and out of consciousness as I heard us speeding through the fallen leaves of the forest. She carried me into a small clearing and waved a hand to magically move a stone slab lying flat on the ground. Under the stone slab lay metal doors. The doors sprang open to reveal a lit stairwell, and she carried me inside. She ran down a corridor to a big round room. There was a pool in the center and three other corridors that led out.

She yelled, "Serena!" Her voice echoed off the stone walls.

A tall redhead ran into the room. A look of shock fell over her when she saw me. "Bring him in here!" she exclaimed as she led us down one corridor.

They hurried me through the first door on the left and placed me on a bed. I could barely hold my eyes open as I tried to stay conscious.

Serena took hold of my wrist to feel the strength of my pulse. "I'll be right back," she told me and ran out of the room.

My elf savior laid her hand on my forehead and closed her eyes. She could feel the blood coursing through my veins. She followed its irregular pulse to my heart to determine my fate.

Serena ran back into the room with a wet towel and a cup filled with a steaming liquid. She handed the towel to the elf, and she took it to wipe the blood from my face. Serena then handed her the drink, but she didn't take it.

"It's too late for that," the elf said as she finished cleaning my face and neck. "He is changing." Great sadness fell over her. "I want to see the life that he has lived."

She handed the bloody towel back to Serena and laid a hand on my forehead again. She closed her eyes to focus. Her hand began to emit a light blue glow as she caught glimpses of my memories. In my weakened state, I couldn't lock my mind from her. As she began to probe my mind, I slipped into the past.

I was running along a creek bank. As I ducked under tree limbs, a fairy sped after me. Being small, she could navigate the trees much easier than I could. She caught up and flew around in front of my face. I stopped and smiled at her. She grabbed my nose with both hands and gave it a quick kiss.

"Tag," she said before giggling and flying straight up into a tree.

I climbed up after her. I saw her fly toward the top and out of sight.

"Kieran, come find me," she said playfully.

I continued up the tree. I climbed within view of the tree top, but I was unable to see her. "Tess?" I called for her. "Tess?" I looked over into an adjacent tree, but she was nowhere to be found. I then heard her giggle. I looked in the direction of where the laughter was coming. I climbed out on all fours onto a branch and found her hiding behind a cluster of leaves. "I found you," I told her.

"You certainly have," she said seductively as she kissed me on my bottom lip.

I did my best to return the kiss.

She placed her hands on both sides of my mouth as she kissed me again. "I wish I were taller," she told me, smiling through a sad tone.

"What if I wish I were smaller?" I asked as we both broke into laughter.

"Oh, I love you," she said with bright eyes and a charming smile.

Before I could open my heart to her, we were interrupted. "Kieran?" my sister called from somewhere below.

Tess and I stopped laughing and quickly began our descent.

"Kieran? We need to get going if we are to watch the sunset," Kelena called out again.

I got in too big of a hurry climbing down, and just before reaching the bottom, I stepped on a bad limb. It broke and I fell.

"KIERAN!" Tess screamed out.

I fell hard on my back. I was conscious but definitely seeing stars.

Kelena ran over to help me. "Kieran, are you okay?" she asked as she held my head up from the mossy creek bank.

Tess flew right up in my face to check on me. "Are you okay?"

I blinked to try and regain focus.

"Kieran? Kieran? Can you hear me?" my sister asked.

I awakened but couldn't quite focus. I could only see silhouettes. I was in pain! "Kelena? TESS!" I yelled.

"Ssshhh, you're okay. You are safe now," the elf said to comfort me.

I breathed deeply as I tried to relax and remember where I was. I was no longer in Sungrove. Kelena had been taken and . . . and Tess was dead. Tess was dead!

My mysterious savior caught quick flashes of the battle with the werewolves and traveled backward through the day. She saw memories of my grandfather. She saw Tess kiss me on the nose. She saw the sunrise from my rooftop. I groaned from pain, so she stopped reading my mind.

"Who are you?" I asked as my eyes began to focus. She was beautiful. Breathtakingly beautiful, I thought to myself. A grin lit her face, and I realized that she was still reading my thoughts. I looked away bashfully, and I saw the one called Serena sitting in a wicker chair at the foot of the bed. I then looked at myself. My shirt had been removed, and I gasped at the sight of my blood-covered body.

"Try to relax," Serena said to me.

I looked at her again and noticed her reptilian eyes. "You are a dragon," I said, relieved. Because dragons were the keepers of the world, all should be set right soon.

"Yes. My name is Serena," she acknowledged with a smile, "and this is Sylvia."

I looked into the eyes of the one standing over me. She was not a dragon. She had shoulder length brown hair and matching eyes. She was gorgeous, and I didn't care if she was reading my thoughts.

A smile broke across her face, and she sent me a telepathic message. *"You are the gorgeous one."* Speaking aloud, she followed with, "We just need to get you cleaned up."

She turned to Serena. "There must be something we can do."

With that, I snapped back to reality, and I was afraid again. I heard over and over in my head, "It's too late for that. He is changing." What's happening to me?

Hearing my thoughts, she could feel my fear, and I saw it overwhelm her.

Serena jumped from the chair and pulled her friend away from me. A pain shot through me like lightning, and my body went cold. Sylvia must have been keeping my brain from registering pain, and now that she wasn't in direct contact with me, I was feeling the full extent of my injuries. I couldn't bear it. It was too much. I lost consciousness.

I awakened to see that it was now Serena that had her hand on my forehead to relieve my pain, and Sylvia was resting in the chair. Serena told me what Sylvia could not bear to. "I'm sorry Kieran, but you are to become a werewolf."

"What? A werewolf! Like the beasts in the forest? I would rather die!"

Sylvia posed a question to Serena. "Do you think my blood can save him?"

Serena thought for a moment while she used her thumb to rub my brow. "Possibly, but we need to give him the choice. He should understand his options and make his own decision on what he wants. Do you think you are ready? Is he the one you would choose?"

Sylvia looked at me lying on the bed. She returned to my side and took Serena's place to magically relieve my pain. I relaxed. Without looking away from me, she answered her friend. "He is the one I want." She then looked at Serena. "And I am ready."

Serena looked at her proudly and lovingly as if Sylvia was her closest, most valued friend. Perhaps they shared a telepathic message because no words were spoken between them.

Sylvia turned to me. "Take long, deep breaths. I'm going to let you see what you will become and what you can become."

I closed my eyes and found myself in a forest. I heard her voice as if it were traveling across a great void. "This will be your life if you choose to do nothing and accept the wolf."

I had thermal vision as well as night vision. I could see the bugs that filled the air. A rabbit sat several yards away. I could see the heat pulsating within its body. I spotted an owl flying through the forest toward the rabbit. I moved closer to scare the rabbit so it would not be caught, and in an instant, I was standing over it. It didn't notice me because I had moved so quickly. I turned my attention to the owl just as it flew into my CLAWS! I finally saw that I was not as I should be. What was this? I dropped the owl.

Sylvia spoke to me, "Since you are so close to death but will not die from the wounds that you suffered from your attacker, you will become like him. I am unsure of the werewolves' beginnings, but some say that it is the possession by a wolf's spirit."

After examining my dark hairy body, I looked down at the owl again and saw that it no longer glowed as it did. It was now as dull as the earth beneath it.

"You are not always in this form," she explained. "Until you learn to control it, you will change every night. As a werewolf, you have heightened senses and much greater speed and strength. Werewolves are immortal creatures, to an extent. They can only be killed by the destruction of their heart or by silver."

I opened my eyes from the vision. "Silver?" I asked, thinking it was an odd thing to be deathly allergic to.

"Yes," Serena answered. "If silver penetrates a werewolf's skin, it will turn its blood into a poison and kill it."

"That's how I killed the one in the forest," Sylvia added. "I had forgotten that the dagger I carried was forged from silver."

I looked at my bloody hands. "Will you use that same dagger on me, so I won't have to live forever as one of those nightmarish creatures?"

Her smile dissipated. "Don't give up on life so easily."

I took a deep breath as I felt tears fill my eyes. "But I have nothing left. My family, my friends, my home, everything that I have ever known has been destroyed. It's all gone."

"You may have lost the life that you lived, but you can start anew." She gave me a warm smile. "Your body is all that you truly own, and I believe it can be fixed. As for your life, could it get any worse?" She didn't wait for me to answer. "It can only get better from here. Now close your eyes, and you will see as I see."

I closed my eyes to find myself once again in the forest. I had the same thermal and night vision as before, but this time, I caught a sweet smell on the wind and spotted three deer. I sped toward them so quickly that they didn't notice me.

Again, from across the void, Sylvia's voice could be heard. "Your speed is greatly increased, but you are not as fast as a werewolf."

I could see faintly glowing veins running through the deer. They finally noticed me and ran. I had no trouble keeping up with them. I reached the edge of the forest just as light began to peek over the horizon. I stopped to see the sunrise with my new vision. The deer ran across an open field toward another forest. I saw the sun, and it burned me. I looked away. My skin was pale white but darkening fast. I ran back into the forest and felt much better in the shade.

"As a vampire, the sun is your enemy," Sylvia told me.

I awakened from the illusion. "I will not be able to see another sunrise?" I asked in disbelief.

"No, you will not," Serena answered. "You cannot let direct sunlight touch you. You must stay shielded from it. The sun's rays will tear down your body and make healing the exposed skin much slower than a regular wound."

"Neither vampires nor werewolves age after being changed," Sylvia cut in to take my thoughts away from never seeing the sun again. "You will look as young as you are now forever. Of course, you can use magic to change your appearance, but this will be your true form."

"The biggest difference between vampires and werewolves," Serena added, "are that vampires gain more mental strength where werewolves gain more physical."

"So which would you rather become?" Sylvia asked me. "You must choose now because the longer you wait, the less chance you will have a choice. Once you have fully changed, there is no turning back."

I looked into Sylvia's big brown eyes but couldn't think for losing myself in them. I turned my eyes to the stone ceiling to weigh my options. I could become a hairy beast, never see the sun again, or die. As much as I would like to get to know Sylvia, I thought I would rather join Tess and my fam . . . KELENA! She was taken! She could still be alive! I must find her. I turned back to Sylvia to give her my answer. "I want to be like you."

She didn't say anything. She rubbed my forehead, and we stared into each other's eyes. She was a gorgeous young elf. She couldn't be more than 200. Well, since she was immortal, I was probably wrong about that. She saved me from dying at the hands, I mean, claws of that monster. Now she was saving me once again from becoming one. She had read my thoughts and was probably still reading them. Having access to my brain, she could know everything about me, and I knew almost nothing about her. She did seem like a genuinely nice person. I would share a sunrise with her. Well, I would if she would not burn up in its light.

Serena broke the silence. "Would you like me

to leave the room?"

Sylvia turned to her. "No. Please stay," she answered as she reached out for Serena's hand. "This is an important moment in my life, in both our lives, and I want you to be here."

Serena took hold of her hand for a moment. "Then I will stay." She stepped over to the side of the room to give us some space.

Sylvia turned her attention back to me, and her eyes sparkled in the magically lit room. "Forget all things and focus on me. Soon, your wounds will be healed, and you will feel more alive than you ever have."

With a hand still on my forehead, she leaned over and breathed in deeply to take in my scent. She rubbed her nose against my cheek and kissed me softly. She climbed on me, and I felt my body tense. The only other woman that I had been that close to was eight inches tall, so I was a little inexperienced at that sort of thing.

I slowly put my arms around her and looked into her lust-filled eyes. She kissed me passionately. I felt her tear my lip as she pulled away, but it didn't hurt. I saw my blood on her mouth. She gave me a smirk and quickly started licking and kissing my face. She bit and pulled at my ear. She then licked my neck before piercing the skin with her teeth. I gasped. Feeling dizzy, I closed my eyes. What was she doing to me? I had already lost a lot of blood, and it felt like she was draining the rest of it from me.

I began to hear two hearts beating. One was slow, and its rhythm was almost hypnotic. The other was irregular. In my mind, I saw Sylvia, and I opened my arms to her.

"You are so beautiful," she told me. "Drink from me, and you will be beautiful forever." A streak of light opened in her mouth. It was like liquid fire on her tongue.

I kissed her, and the light began to pour into my mouth. It was warm and thick. Her tongue slid between my lips so I could get more. Her mouth went dark as another streak of red light opened on the side of her neck. I moved to it and began drinking. My heart beat faster as I squeezed her for more and more.

"Yes, take it all," she ordered.

I reached up to pull her hair from my face and noticed that my hand was glowing. My hands and arms were emitting a golden glow. I gasped and pulled my mouth away from Sylvia's neck to look at myself, but it was gone. I was no longer glowing.

Sylvia was sucking on my neck just as I was hers. She slowly pulled away and told me, "Don't stop. Drink more."

I looked at her neck to see that there really was a cut on it, and not red light but blood was oozing from it. I put my tongue to it and quickly remembered the taste. I licked the thick blood off her neck and covered the slice with my mouth. She licked at my neck before sucking on it again. I was covered with sweat and dried blood but continued to drain her. She took blood from me as I took blood from her. Our bodies pulsed in unison until we could drink no more.

I saw the slice on her neck quickly heal shut. I felt her lick at my neck and kiss my ear. She rose and looked at me with pleasured eyes. She kissed me softly on the lips.

My breathing quickened. Starting at my feet, paralysis worked its way up my body. What was going on? I was dying! I was dying! I tried to scream but couldn't. My vision blurred, and everything went black.

I must have been out only mere moments because I awoke to find Sylvia resting her head on my chest, listening to my heartbeat.

"Welcome to immortality," she said with a smile.

Serena stood. I had forgotten she was still in the room. She stepped over and kissed us both on the forehead before leaving the room.

"Why me?" I finally asked. "Why give me this gift when we have just met?"

"I have glimpsed your past and studied your thoughts," she answered. "I have felt love as you feel it. You are so special, and you have so much potential."

We lay quietly together until Serena returned. Her footsteps could be heard coming down the corridor to the room. She stopped in the doorway. "I have prepared a bath for you," she said to me and turned to head back toward the central chamber.

Sylvia stood and offered a hand to me. "Even through the pain and loss you have endured tonight, I can see that you are truly a beautiful person, inside and out, Kieran of Sungrove."

I took her hand and stood up from the bed. I felt rested. I felt refreshed and yet dirty.

"Come on," she added with a smile. "Let's get you cleaned up," she said as if she was still reading my thoughts. She led me down the corridor.

I breathed in deeply the smell of flowers in the room. There was a pool in the center, and it was covered with an array of colorful flower petals. I looked at the pool and then to Sylvia and Serena.

Sylvia began to snicker a bit. "What do you want us to do, turn around?"

I blushed but laughed it off. "I am a bit shy," I confessed.

Sylvia and Serena laughed as they turned around so I could undress and ease into the steaming hot water. It was deep enough to come up around my shoulders. I began washing away the dried blood from my body.

Sylvia sat at the edge of the pool to wash the blood from her face and arms that had stained her while lying with me.

Serena picked up my ruined clothes and dropped them in a basket. She placed a set of fresh clothing and a pair of sandals next to the pool.

Sylvia finished washing up and watched me for a moment before speaking. "I'm sorry about your friend, Tess," she said sadly.

I stopped washing for a moment and stared at the water.

Sylvia lowered her head, unable to look at me. "You loved her?" Her voice was almost a whisper, like it pained her to ask.

I nodded my head. "Yes. She was my first love."

There was silence between us for a moment. I sighed heavily and continued my bath.

Sylvia finally looked at me. It was hard for her to hold back her emotions. She seemed truly sorry for what I had gone through tonight. Being immortal, she must know what it's like to lose a loved one.

"Once you get cleaned up," she began, "we will see if we can track down where your sister was taken."

"I won't be much longer," I answered as I scratched the dried blood out from under my nails. I saw that all my wounds had healed. There was no sign of a bite mark on my shoulder. As I examined my body, noticing that I had no scars what-so-ever, I felt a terrible hunger pang. "I'm hungry," I told Sylvia, who brought me a towel and held it up, so I could step out of the pool without being embarrassed.

"We'll grab a bite on the way," she said with a laugh.

Sylvia led me and Serena to where she found me in the forest. The body of the elf that could transform into a wolf was lying face down, naked in the dirt.

Serena found the werewolf's tracks and ran her finger along the edge of it.

"How did you find me out here?" I asked Sylvia.

Without looking at me, she answered, "I was out hunting and caught the sound of battle on the wind. As I followed the sound, I began to smell smoke. I came upon a city in ruin. The fires had already been rained out; only smoldering heaps remained. I picked up the same trail that you had, and I followed."

I looked back at the elf's body and squatted down next to it to get a closer look at the fingernails. I found no sign that this elf had ever been a large, bloodthirsty beast.

Sylvia saw me examining the body. "Why would a couple of werewolves be out here in the middle of nowhere?" she asked Serena. "For what purpose would Sungrove be destroyed?"

Serena thought for a moment as she watched me examine the body. "Maybe I can try something," she said finally. She knelt next to the body and put her hands on both sides of its head. She closed her eyes to concentrate. Her hands glowed blue as she gained access to his fading memories.

His name was Jacob. She saw flashes of Sylvia fighting him to save Kieran. She went back further to see the houses of Sungrove being torched by two Dark Elves while stone golems stomped through the city, smashing elves with their huge fists. One of the Dark Elves was a warlock named Byron. The other was his apprentice, Veronica.

Serena flashed backward again through his memories to see five horsemen entering the city. Their horses were rotten beneath rusty armor. The horsemen removed their hoods and began their attack. Byron and Veronica cast spells to create stone golems from nearby boulders. Jacob and the other horseman dismounted and transformed into werewolves. The fifth horseman, a vampire named Dirk, joined them in killing the elves of Sungrove.

Yuri ran out to face the two spellcasters. He transformed into his true form, which was a Yellow Dragon. He swung his tail to destroy two of the golems. The debris was knocked toward Byron and Veronica, but they threw up a magical barrier to protect themselves. He inhaled and breathed fire at them, but Byron cast a barrier that protected them from the intense heat. He strained to keep the shield up. Veronica held out a glass orb. A bubble formed around Yuri, and it began floating toward the orb. It gradually shrank as it got closer, making Yuri smaller. When it touched the orb, it popped inside, trapping Yuri within the orb.

The peaceful elves of Sungrove didn't stand a chance against two spellcasters, two werewolves, and a vampire. They were killed and incinerated. Serena pulled away from the body.

"What did you see?" Sylvia asked.

Serena, almost in tears, looked at me but didn't say a word. I knew by the look on her face that no one survived the attack. The strength in my legs began to give way, but Sylvia ran over and caught me before I fell. She eased me to the ground where I cried tears of blood in her arms. While holding me close, Sylvia asked Serena, "Did you see where they went?"

Serena placed her hands back on Jacob's head. She searched quickly through the fading memories to find a castle built on the side of a volcano. The memories led her inside to find Sungrove's attackers receiving their orders from their ruler sitting on a throne of bones. The large room looked like a slaughter house and reeked of decay. The bodies of elves were nailed to the walls and hung by hooks from the ceiling. A table of bloody instruments sat next to the throne. It appeared as if he had captured and tortured these elves until he learned the location of Sungrove. The brutal ruler flashed sharp fangs through an evil grin. Serena let go of Jacob to sever the link to his memories, and she looked back to Sylvia with horror in her eyes.

CHAPTER IV

AN ANCIENT AWAKENS

Outside her underground home, Sylvia and I practiced fighting techniques. We stood next to each other, facing the west as the sky grew violet with the fall of the sun. I was studying her from the corner of my eye and mimicking her every move. I learned the form and no longer had to watch her. We practiced in time with one another and gradually sped up.

She stopped and turned to me. "Now that you know the moves, you must understand them."

She attacked me. I blocked the first attack, but she tagged me with the second. We continued for several moments. I became increasingly harder to hit. I finally caught her with an open palm to the chest that knocked her back.

"Very good," she congratulated me with a smile. "You are a quick learner. All right, now you need a weapon. Think of creating an extension of your arm in the form of a blade." She held her right fist up, and a 2' transparent blade appeared. "It's an ethereal blade. You summon it like you would a spirit, and it performs as you believe it should," she explained.

I held my right fist up in the same manner and concentrated on it. "We can't just use a regular sword?" I asked with a hint of sarcasm.

"Normal weapons can't withstand our strength," she answered, "and I don't think you want your sword to break in the middle of battle." She met my sarcasm with a bit of her own.

"Good point," I said with a smile before concentrating again. I stared intensely at my fist but couldn't seem to cast the spell. I looked back at Sylvia's blade and noticed a strange, otherworldly smoke coming from it. The blade actually looked like a ghost. "From where does the smoke come?" I asked.

She looked at her ethereal blade. "I've been told that it comes from another plane of existence, a plane that we cannot perceive. That is all I know. I must say, magic is not my forte. I only know a little to get me by."

I now understood a little better of what I was trying to create. I concentrated again on summoning the ethereal blade and succeeded. The magical blade extended from my fist, and wisps of ethereal smoke came forth. Both Sylvia and I smiled.

"Great. You did it," she congratulated me.

Serena walked out of the open stairwell of their home. "I can't come with you," she told us.

Our weapons dissipated.

"But we need your help," Sylvia pleaded.

"I must report the attack on Sungrove to the World Council," Serena explained. Her eyes said that she would much rather come with us.

"Very well," Sylvia said with a sigh. "Kieran and I will join you once we have rescued Yuri and his sister."

Serena walked over to give me a hug. I felt warm in her arms, warmer than being in Sylvia's arms. It must be the difference in body temperature between vampires and dragons.

She kissed me on the forehead. "Be careful," she said to me, "both of you." She then hugged Sylvia for a long moment and kissed her forehead.

Sylvia returned the kiss. "We will."

"Then I will see you both soon," Serena said just before leaping straight up. Once she cleared the tree tops, red leathery wings sprang out from her back, and she flew away.

Even though Serena was out of sight, Sylvia watched the sky for a few moments more, perhaps with hope she would return. She then turned to me, took a combative stance, and smiled. I moved in to show her what I've learned. We fought, and it didn't take long for me to take her off balance. As she was falling, she grabbed hold of me, causing me to fall with her. I landed on top of her, and we both laughed. "I think we're ready to go save your sister," she said to me.

I ran my fingers through her hair as I got trapped in her big, brown eyes.

"We can continue with this once we return," she told me, giving me a soft kiss on the nose.

I stood and helped her to her feet. "We better get going then," I said.

With a wave of her hand, the doors to the sanctuary closed, and the large stone slab slid over them. I followed her east with unnatural speed. Through forests and over mountains, we ran. We zipped by animals so quickly that they had no time to react. We even ran through an ogre encampment, but they passed us off as the light from their campfires playing tricks on their eyes.

Sylvia and I reached the edge of a great forest just as the first rays of sunlight splashed over a castle. It was the same castle that Serena saw in Jacob's mind. It had been built on the side of a volcano. The weeds had grown high, and trees dotted the side.

Following my normal morning routine, I glanced at the sunrise but quickly remembered that I must break that routine when my eyes began burning. I turned away and threw my hood up. Sylvia already had the hood of her cloak pulled up. She turned me around to take a look at my eyes. I was more mentally hurt than physically hurt that I couldn't watch the sunrise. My lashes were burned away, and my eyes were a smoky color. I closed them just as she kissed my lids.

We walked across a grassy field to the foot of the volcano. I noticed that there were no birds singing that morning. I heard nothing but the sound of our footsteps through the tall grass. The only other time that I remembered nature being that quiet was just before being attacked by werewolves.

We stepped onto a rocky trail and followed it up the side of the volcano to the large double doors of the castle. Sylvia took hold of one of the door handles but let go before trying to open it. She looked up to the nearest window. "Let's enter from that window," she pointed.

She jumped to the window ledge, which was about twenty feet up, and peeked in to make sure it was clear before entering. I jumped to the ledge and followed her inside. We paused to listen for any signs of life within the castle. The dank smell of mildew filled my nostrils. We heard nothing. I felt uneasy about this, but I must find Kelena. I must save my sister.

This room used to be a bedchamber. The wood was rotten, and the linen had long since deteriorated.

My footing slipped as I stepped forward. Sylvia quickly covered her mouth to stifle a snicker. I'm glad I had on sandals because the stone floor was slick with mold. I carefully stepped toward the open door and found that the mold didn't cover the entire floor. It seemed to be caused from rain blowing in through the open window. There were no longer shutters to keep out the wind and rain.

I followed Sylvia out of the room, and we quietly walked down the hallway. We peered into the other rooms that lined the hall, but we found no signs of life. It seemed to be a deserted castle.

We followed a staircase that led down to another long hallway lined with rooms. We continued to glance into rooms as we passed but still found nothing. The hall led into a large room. It was the castle's main entrance. Just inside the castle doors stood two 10' tall, beautifully cut marble statues of armored knights. Their deep etchings had made wonderful homes for funnel-web spiders. The carcasses of the spider's meals surrounded the statues rusty iron bases.

Sylvia and I crossed the room to another hall. We took a few steps down the hall before hearing a heavy pounding sound. I peered into the room that we had just passed through. A fist came crashing down at my head! I barely had time to move out of the way of it. Another fist swung toward me, but Sylvia pulled me back into the hallway.

The two marble statues, which were really marble golems that guarded the castle entrance, followed us into the hall. Sylvia and I could barely dodge the endless attacks from them. Sylvia pushed me back as she summoned an ethereal blade. She swung her blade up to defend against an attack, and she cut through the wrist of one of the golems. The hand dropped heavily behind her.

An army of skeletons and zombies flooded the other end of the hall, so I concentrated on summoning a blade of my own. As they got closer, I noticed that they all had solid black eyes.

Sylvia cut off the right arm of the other golem, and she stepped into me as she tried to back away from them.

I yelled out over the golem's thundering attacks, "We can't go this way either!"

She took a quick glance behind her and saw the approaching undead. She stepped between the two golems. One of the golems threw a punch at her, but she ducked, and it punched the other golem's stomach. Hairline fractures ran through its torso.

"Come on!" she yelled at me.

I hurried toward her. She grabbed my hand and pulled me between the golems. We ran back to the castle's entrance only to be surrounded by an army of skeleton warriors, zombies, and bone golems. The army had apparently come from the other hall. Sylvia and I fought back to back for a few moments.

Fallen skeleton warriors reattached themselves and came back to fight again. Zombies kept coming until we cleaved their brains.

I noticed Sylvia had fallen behind me. She had been knocked unconscious by a bone golem. The 8' tall mass of human and animal bones were held together by rotting flesh and muscles. It had two legs and four arms. There were skulls scattered throughout its body, and they all seemed to be studying me. Its eyes were solid black like the rest of the undead surrounding us, but this time, I noticed something that I didn't before. There was a face of an old, white-haired Dark Elf staring at me through those eyes. The bone golem grabbed me by the arms, pulled me forward and slammed a fist into the side of my head.

I regained consciousness to find myself inside a bubble. Sylvia and I were held captive in individual bubbles that were draining our energy and sending the energy to a magical orb that powered our prisons. The orb sat on a pedestal in the center of the otherwise bare room.

I lay in my floating prison, staring at the floor. My body was on fire with the thirst. "I need blood!" My body's scream for blood was deafening, but only a whisper escaped my lips. It was agony, consciousness without mobility. I scratched at the clear wall of my prison, but even the simplest movement was hard to accomplish. I could not escape.

I looked over to Sylvia as we slowly spun around the room. She looked weak but continued to cast spells against her prison. Every spell seemed to only feed the center orb.

I then got the idea to absorb the energy from the orb itself. I needed to make my body into a sponge for magical energies. I used every ounce of my remaining strength to outstretch my hand toward the magical orb. My eyes rolled back into my head as I began to pull the energy from the orb. Blue lightning flowed through the wall of my bubble prison with an electrical buzz as it met my fingertips. It was working! I could feel the energy revitalizing me.

Just as our prisons began to fade, Byron's apprentice, Veronica walked into the room. She saw what I was doing and ran toward the magical orb. She took it from the pedestal and drew the energy back from me. A devilish grin cracked her unnaturally beautiful face. "Trying to escape, are we?" she asked. It sounded like two voices speaking in unison. One was sexually arousing while the other sounded ghostly. She rubbed her hand across my prison as she passed by, starring into my eyes. "You're very clever. You would make an excellent apprentice. It's a pity you must burn."

Sylvia and I unwillingly followed her down a long corridor and down a wide spiraling stairwell. The stairs opened into a large chamber. We were inside the volcano!

The warlock, Byron stood at the edge of the volcanic chasm with the orb that powered Yuri's prison in his hands. An opened book floated before him. Yuri was positioned over the chasm.

Byron was the Dark Elf that I saw in the eyes of the undead! He must have had control of them, his own personal army, created by him, to do his bidding.

We stood on a rim of rock that lined about one third of the volcano's circumference.

Veronica gave a slight bow to a pale, middle-aged man. "Artimes," she greeted him. "Here are the two intruders."

Artimes walked over with Dirk to view me and Sylvia, held within our prisons. "Yes, thank you, Veronica."

Dirk stared at me. "This is the twin, milord," he told Artimes. "He has come to rescue his sister," he said with sarcasm as I had no doubt failed in my attempt.

Artimes looked at me again as he gave Dirk a command. "Bring her down to witness his demise. She will be my eternal slave or suffer the same fate."

"Yes, milord." Dirk bowed to him before speeding up the stairs.

Byron looked up. "It is time," he said aloud.

Everyone, including me, looked up to see that the moon had completely covered the mouth of the volcano.

Byron studied over a page in his book before speaking again, but this time, his voice was not of an old man's; it thundered from deep within him as if he could command nature herself. "BY THE LIGHT OF THE MOON AND THE BLOOD OF A YELLOW DRAGON, I, OF STRONG MIND AND HEART, BREAK THE SEAL CREATED MILLENNIA AGO TO HOLD MAGNUS THE RED WITHIN THE EARTH."

Sylvia and I watched in horror as Yuri's bubble prison burst, and he plummeted to a fiery grave. The volcano rumbled with the breaking of the powerful spell.

Veronica then stepped next to Byron. She used her orb to steer me and Sylvia over the pit. Sylvia and I pressed a hand against our prison walls and looked at each another one last time.

"I love you," her lips said to me as her prison dissipated.

I screamed, "NO!" but my voice couldn't escape the prison. I saw her fall into the darkness below me. I closed my eyes, expecting my prison to burst, but it didn't. I looked over to Veronica and the other witnesses of my coming death, and I saw Kelena being held by a leash.

Tears streamed down her face. She turned to look at the one who held her. Her muscles tensed as dark red hair started to cover her fair, elvish skin. Her keeper sent lightning through the leash. Her back arched, and she screamed out as she was shocked into submission. She collapsed to the ground and returned to her elf form. She looked at me with defeated eyes.

Before Veronica released me, Dirk spoke up. "I want to be the one to send him to his doom."

Veronica held the orb out for him to take. With excitement on his face, he hurried over.

The volcano continued to rumble like it could erupt at any moment.

Dirk's expression went cold as he stared at me. "It's a pity you have to die before you've learned anything."

I turned my eyes to Kelena, who was just as

powerless as I.

Dirk began to chuckle as his thoughts amused him. "Don't worry; I'll send her down shortly."

My prison burst, and I began the long fall into the abyss. His laughter faded as the darkness enveloped me, and the warmth radiating from below eased my weakened body to sleep.

"Kieran?" my mother called. She dropped to her knees so she could be eye level with me. "Kieran, look at me." She lifted my chin. Tears were streaming down my face. "Everything will be okay," she told me with a glistening tear in her eye. She looked young for a moment, like a little girl again.

Sniffling back a runny nose, "Why did grandfather have to die?" I looked past her to see Kelena having the same conversation with our father.

She touched the tears from my face and sighed deeply as she tried to hold back her own feelings for the passing of her father. "He was ready to see your grandmother again," she told me.

Hesitantly I asked, "Did he kill himself?"

She looked away and wiped her eyes, unable to hold back her sorrow. For the first time, I caught a glimpse of someone's thoughts. I could see her imagining her father standing alone at his spot on the mountain. He was speaking to grandmother with tears streaming down his face. He set fire to his clothing and jumped to his death. His spirit left his body, and he raced toward the Sun. It was hot. The Sun was so very hot.

I woke up to find that I was still falling, and the cavern was glowing red from the light of the volcanic magma. My skin was burning! I was burning! This was it! "I'm sorry Kelena. I have failed you."

Flames reached up to catch me, but they took the form of a woman with wings. As I was lifted up the chasm, I watched this fiery, flying woman become Sylvia with golden wings. I saw determination on her face as she sped toward the surface.

"Are you taking us to the Sun?"

Without looking at me, she answered, "We're not dead."

The wall of the volcano began to break and crumble. She zipped around falling rocks with ease. The light from the chamber where we were dropped came into view. When we reached the chamber, she tossed me to solid ground, away from our enemies. She screamed out as her skin ignited. With the castle crumbling around us, she began her attack. She threw fire at her closest enemies, Veronica and Artimes. Veronica had reclaimed the magic orb from Dirk but dropped it as she flailed, trying to extinguish the flames. Sylvia caught the orb before it shattered upon the ground.

Artimes leaped at her in an attempt to take back the orb, but she hit him with a fireball. Dirk saved him from the fire by smothering it out with his cloak and carried him out of the cavern before the volcano erupted.

Sylvia used the orb to create barriers around everyone. The barrier cut through the magical leash, separating Kelena from her keeper.

With his book tucked under his arm, Byron used the orb that he had to create another barrier around himself.

"Kelena!" I yelled.

Sylvia released her and threw the orb into the chasm. The prisoners followed the orb into the volcano.

As the castle crumbled, Sylvia put her arms around us and flew out of the volcano. She landed at the edge of the forest.

Kelena and I hugged each other. "I'm so glad you're okay," we said in unison.

The volcano erupted, and we watched in disbelief as an enormous Red Dragon climbed out of it. The lava ran off him as he stretched. He then breathed fire high into the sky. In a low rumbling voice, the dragon spoke. "I have awakened. I, Magnus, have finally risen from the depths of the Earth."

Sylvia grabbed hold of us again and took to the air. We flew east over forests and vast deserts.

Hidden away in the mountains, we landed outside a magnificent palace constructed of marble and gold. Sylvia's wings folded away and faded from sight. With invisible hands, she opened the huge double doors. We stepped inside the palace, and we were greeted by two green-haired elves.

"Welcome to the World Council Palace," one of the elves said. "How may we be of assistance?"

"We are here to see Serena the Red," Sylvia told them.

"This way, please," the elves said in unison as they turned to lead us to Serena's room.

The palace didn't have steps to get between

floors. It had a wide spiraling walkway. There was an empty void up the center and a skylight at the top. There were also three columns of vertical glass that ran the height of the palace walls.

The elves led us up to one of the many rooms in the palace. One elf knocked twice on the door. We heard Serena say, "You may enter." The elf opened the door, and we found Serena writing in a book. She immediately ran into Sylvia's arms. "I've missed you."

"And I have missed you," Sylvia whispered.

Serena then gave my sister a hug. "Kelena, I'm glad you're safe. My name is Serena."

"Thank you," Kel said to her.

Serena gave me a hug and kissed me on the forehead. "I have already told the council leader what I know of the destruction of Sungrove. You need to inform him of what has happened since."

"I will," I told her.

"The council will be having a meeting at midday," Serena told us. "You and Kelena should attend."

"Won't you and Sylvia be joining us?" I asked.

"Serena and I have some things to discuss," Sylvia answered.

Serena looked at her inquisitively but said nothing.

CHAPTER V

THE WORLD COUNCIL

Kelena and I were escorted to the council chamber by the two green-haired elves. The chamber was one of the top level rooms in the palace.

Six dragon lords, in the form of elves, sat at a long table in a large room. There was a representative for each of the major dragon species. Only the color of their hair and eyes hinted at their true form.

A white-haired male stood from the head of the table and walked over to us. "Kieran and Kelena, welcome to the World Council Palace. I am Ian the White, head of the council," he said with a smile as he offered me the peaceful greeting with his hands out, palms up.

I placed my hands, palms down on his, and we both bowed our heads slightly. "Thank you," I told him before stepping aside to let Kelena greet him.

"We are glad to see you have escaped your captors," Ian said to her with a warm smile.

"Thank you."

Ian then motioned to a couple of empty chairs at the table, "Please, if you will."

We took our seats.

"Now, if everyone will introduce themselves to our guests, we can continue with the meeting," he told everyone.

A tall, blonde woman stood from the opposite end of the table from Ian. "Good day to you, Kieran and Kelena. I am Ariana the Yellow. We are sorry to hear of the destruction of Sungrove. You have our deepest sympathy."

A woman with very long, green hair stood to greet us. "I am Mya the Green. I hope you enjoy your stay here at the palace."

The council member sitting next to me stood to introduce herself. I found her strangely beautiful with her short, blue hair and cerulean blue eyes. "My name is Gwyneth," she said to me with a smile, "representative for the Blue Dragons. It is nice to meet you."

The council greetings had reached Ian, so he motioned for the member to his left to continue.

Sitting across from Kel was a strong, dark-haired male. His eyes looked strange, being only black and white. He stood to greet us. "Good day, young ones," he said with a bow. "I am Kildren, Kildren the Black."

A dark red-haired man with glowing red eyes stood. "I am Drakuss, representative for the Red Dragons," he said proudly. "We are all pleased to meet you, Kieran and Kelena of Sungrove. If there is anything that we can do to make your stay more enjoyable, please do not hesitate to ask."

"Thank you," Kel and I said in unison.

"Good," Ian said as he sat forward, clasping his hands together. "Now we can move on with the meeting. Kieran, Serena has informed us of everything up until you and Sylvia left to rescue Kelena. Please tell us of what you learned within the castle where she was being held."

Everyone's attention was focused on me as I stared at the table to focus my thoughts. "A vampire named Artimes sent a group to Sungrove to capture Yuri the Yellow. I believe he targeted Yuri specifically because he was young and could easily be captured. Artimes' castle was built on the side of a volcano where a powerful warlock sacrificed Yuri to break a spell holding Magnus the Red within the core of the Earth."

"And you saw this Red Dragon?" Drakuss asked.

"Yes, we saw him climb out of the volcano," I answered.

The double doors to the council chamber opened, and six elves walked in single file bringing lunch to the council members. They each carried a different dish, and I took notice of who was having what.

The lovely Gwyneth was having shrimp with white wine. Mya was having venison with red wine. Ariana was having mahi mahi with white wine. Drakuss was having steak with a goblet of blood. Ian was having a human brain from a severed head with a goblet of blood. Kildren was eating alligator with a goblet of blood.

As the waiters began leaving the room, Ian stopped one of them. "Wait just a moment," he ordered. Ian then looked at me and Kel, "Would you like something?" he asked us, but he didn't wait for an answer. "Bring our guests a drink," he commanded the waiter as he lifted his goblet.

"Right away, milord," the waiter said with a bow before hurrying out of the room.

As I watched everyone begin their lunch, I noticed characteristics about them. Ariana and Gwyneth showed a bit more class than the others, where Drakuss, Mya, and Kildren seemed relaxed. Ian looked eager to continue with the meeting.

I knew that the council members must have been well over 1,000 years old, but they had chosen to take the form of elves in the prime of their lives. They reflected the perfect balance of wisdom and youth.

Gwyneth dabbed her lips with a napkin before speaking. "How could we not know that there was an ancient dragon held prisoner within the Earth?" She was so elegant and proper.

Ian, the most powerful of the dragons and leader of the World Council, voiced his thoughts on the matter. "He must have been imprisoned before any of us became council members."

Drakuss posed another question, "Then why were we not told by the former members?"

Before Ian could answer, Mya spoke up. "Perhaps they did not know."

At that very moment, the doors opened, but it wasn't the waiter bringing drinks. It was a human! He had dark red hair, nails, and eyes. "Or perhaps the council didn't want you to know," he said to follow up Mya's answer to Drakuss' question.

Everyone stood from the table. The stranger motioned for us to sit. "Please," he said to us, but no one sat.

Ian breathed deeply and stepped over to him. He offered him the peaceful greeting. "You must be Magnus the Red," he presumed.

The stranger replied to the greeting by putting his hands, palms down on Ian's and giving him a smirk. "Yes, I am Magnus."

They nodded slightly to each other. Everyone, including Ian, took their seats. Magnus slowly walked around the room as he looked over the World Council members.

"Why would the former council members not want us to know that you were being held prisoner within the Earth?" Ariana asked Magnus as he walked along the opposite end of the table behind Ian. If there could be a queen of the World Council, of the entire world for that matter, Ariana would be her. Being the tallest of the council members at 5'9", she was wildly beautiful. With her long, golden locks, and her sun kissed skin, entire civilizations would fall at the bat of her lashes.

"I was once one of the chair holders of the World Council," Magnus said as he continued around the table, "but all of that changed when I acted on a plan that the other members did not agree on. Now I have a new council to present my plan to, and I do hope you see things differently than your prede-cessors."

Ian motioned for Magnus to go on with his

speech.

"I foresee a future where humans inhabit the entire planet," Magnus explained. "They follow one set of rules written by one government that its members have been chosen to make decisions for the entire human race."

Without letting Magnus continue, Mya rudely interrupted. "So you were imprisoned for your stupidity," she stated, showing her edgy personality.

"We can't grant that kind of power to the humans," Ariana explained. "They will make decisions for all."

"And that would lead to a war of the races," Kelena added.

"The humans will only think they are in control," Magnus explained with a proud smile. He obviously loved his plan. "We will take human form and hold the highest positions of their government," he continued, "or persuade their leaders to make the decisions that we see fit."

Ariana still thought that Magnus' plan would create more problems than it would solve. "Showing favoritism toward the humans will still cause tension among the races," she told him.

Magnus directed his vision of the future directly to Ariana instead of the entire council as he had been. "The planet's population is growing. The space between territories is depleting. War is unavoidable."

"Then what do you propose we do?" Ian asked to bring Magnus' focus on him.

"I propose we fight the war for them," Magnus answered.

The dragon lords were furious. All the council members voiced their opinion, but no one voice could be singled out from the others.

Realizing that nothing was being heard through all that was being said, the council members grew quiet.

Drakuss the Red was the first to speak out. "For this plan to work, the other races will need to be completely eliminated," he said with a look of confusion.

"We cannot do this!" Ian exclaimed with a pound of his fist. He couldn't believe such a plan would even be presented to the World Council.

"How could eradicating entire races even be an option?" Mya asked, believing Magnus was an idiot.

"The humans will eventually outnumber and destroy them anyway," Magnus answered, keeping his cool. "We will just be helping things move along."

"Then why not just let things move along on their own?" Gwyneth asked. Siding with natural selection, she must be a purist.

Magnus spoke directly to her, voicing that he didn't share her beliefs. "If you already know the inevitable outcome, why not help it along?"

"The dragons cannot possibly win a war against so many," Mya admitted.

"We will only need to eliminate four races," Magnus explained. "They are the ones that cannot conceal themselves from the humans but . . . we must destroy all signs that they had ever existed."

"Why make such drastic changes to the world for a race of pitiful beings?" Kildren asked, trying to make sense of it all.

Magnus stood behind Kelena. For once, he showed a sign of emotion but only for a moment. He was saddened at humans being labeled as pitiful beings. He took a breath before speaking. "One reason is that the human population is growing much faster than the others because they are having more offspring in a shorter amount of time." Everyone was quiet as they studied Magnus. They saw that he actually cared for the humans.

"The humans will outnumber all the other races combined within just a few hundred years," Gwyneth said in a low tone as if she thought aloud to better understand what Magnus was saying.

I had been sitting quietly during the entire meeting, listening and taking in all that was said. Now that the tension in the room had eased a little, I decided to speak and pose a question which suggested a peaceful solution to the world's problem. "Instead of destroying four races to help one, why not help them all in existing together?"

Everyone turned their attention to me, but they remained quiet.

Kelena followed up with the answer to my question, but she directed it toward everyone. "We can start by promoting trade among the races to help build friendships. With friendships forged, there will be no war."

Ariana smiled at such a loving answer. "If only it were that easy."

"The races have divided," Drakuss told us, "claimed territories and are not friendly to outsiders."

"Most of them do not even accept outsiders of their own kind," Mya added. "They do not want to trade. They make it, or they take it."

The room was quiet for a moment; everyone seemed lost in their own thoughts.

"So do we all agree on what needs to be done?" Magnus asked, breaking the silence. He believed the council was closer to accepting his plan for world reform.

"No, we do not," Ian's voice rang out as the final say in the matter.

Everyone looked at Ian, but no one showed signs that they were for or against Magnus' plan. They then looked at Magnus to see his reaction.

Magnus took a deep breath. "Then what do you propose we do about the increasing threat of world war?" he asked Ian calmly.

"The council will grant permanent territories to the races," Ian answered.

"If the world is divided among the races," Magnus warned, "we will be on constant alert in keeping the peace."

Ian stood, keeping his palms on the table to show that his decision also stood. "We will do whatever it takes to keep the peace among the races. We will not slaughter hundreds of thousands of creatures and beings just so the humans will think that they have the world to themselves."

"Very well," Magnus said, smiling through defeat. He walked over to look out one of the large windows at dark clouds covering the sky. "But my vision of the future will become reality." He turned back to Ian. "Whether the council supports it or not," he added before leaving the room.

Gwyneth spoke up. "How shall we react if

Magnus proceeds with his plan to reform the planet?"

"Without the approval of the council," Drakuss answered, "it will be difficult for Magnus to organize an army strong enough to win a war against entire races."

"His confidence suggests that he does not need approval," I pointed out as everyone turned to me because of my disturbing observation.

CHAPTER VI

SYLVIA'S PAST

I sat up from a bed of blankets and pillows that we had spread out on the floor. "Because you caught glimpses of my memories while caring for me, I feel as if you know everything about me," I explained. "I'm interested in hearing about you. I would like to know the life you lived before you were given immortality."

Sylvia sat up and draped a blanket over her bare shoulders to cover herself. She held out her wrist for me to drink from it.

I pushed her hand down. "I rather you tell me. I want to hear your voice."

She looked at me inquisitively. "But you can gain access to my memories through my blood, or whatever it is that courses through me now, and know everything about me in mere moments," she pointed out.

"Yes, I know," I told her, "but we are immortal. Why must we rush through things when we will live forever?"

"Very well." She thought for a moment where to begin her story. "I was born in Magestice, 976 years ago."

"Wow!" I exclaimed. "I had no idea you were that old!"

Giving me a dirty look, I immediately realized she didn't like me calling her old. "I'm sorry to interrupt you. Please, continue," I apologized.

"I grew up like any other elf in Magestice," she continued. "I helped my family around our home. I went to school with my two brothers. I didn't hold much interest in magic, even though Magestice has a wonderful school. Elves from all over the world came to study the most powerful of spells. After the fundamental classes, my best friend and I decided to continue our education in the study of the harmony of life."

"She became interested in a boy in our class, and they spent ever-increasing time together. She tried setting me up with one of his friends so we could go out as couples, but I was very particular. Eventually, she gave up trying to find me a mate as she thought more about her future with hers. I tried to convince her otherwise, but they decided to quit school to follow a group setting out to develop a new city. I hated to see her go since she was my only friend, but I promised her that I will follow once I finished school. With my best friend gone and several years of school ahead of me, I spent most of my time deep in study so I would graduate early."

The blanket draped over her shoulders began to slide off. She broke from her story to pull it back into place.

"Thank you," I told her with a smile. "I would hate for your womanly form to distract me from your story," I said sarcastically.

She laughed at the remark. "Oh, you are quite welcome. I wouldn't want my words to go unheard."

We laughed for a moment longer before she continued. "One day, while I was doing research in the library, I was approached by a Dark Elf who introduced himself as Ambros. He was going to school for Necromancy and Transmutation. At first, he seemed a bit creepy, but his quirky personality and quick wit soon put me at ease. Because of this, I felt unusually comfortable with him, and we soon became friends. I noticed that he had an extreme sensitivity to sunlight, but I never asked him about it. I knew he would tell me when he was ready, and he did."

"He was a vampire," I thought aloud.

"Yes," she confirmed. "He told me that he used to be a vampire hunter until he was captured. As a sadistic joke, he was turned into one. He told me that there are many kinds of vampires and that he had come to Magestice in hopes of understanding the transformation process and perhaps create a cure. For his experiments, he needed someone that was not a vampire, so I volunteered. We raced on foot to compare our speed. He recorded the maximum amount of weight that we could lift. He compared the height and distance that we could jump. He tested our sight, smell, and hearing. He also compared how well we learn different subjects such as math, science, languages, and magic."

"What were the results?" I asked.

"We found that he was physically weaker during the day but still able to outperform me in almost every test," she answered. "I did have better vision during the daylight hours, but he didn't expect to find so much potential in being a vampire. He saw life from their point of view, and it wasn't as bad as he once thought. He realized that vampirism was more of a blessing than a curse, and he had his findings printed clearly on parchment."

"Next, he wanted to study the actual transformation process as it happens, and I was the most logical candidate. After seeing how powerful I could be as a vampire, I didn't have to be asked twice."

"How did your family react when they saw you after becoming a vampire?" I asked her. "Did you tell them what you had become?"

"No!" she exclaimed. "No, I never told them. They thought maybe all my time studying in the library was taking its toll on me. I looked sickly, so I had to assure them that I was fine. I told Ambros that we should try to blend in a little better, so he found an illusion spell to help us. It seemed to have worked since my family mentioned that I looked healthier. I told them that, with graduation coming up, I felt as if a heavy burden was lifting off my shoulders."

"Which was the truth," I stated.

"Yes, it was the truth," she assured me. "It had been almost ten years since I last saw my childhood friend. We had kept in touch by messenger only. Now that I had finished school, I talked Ambros into going with me to see her. I wasn't planning to move, but at least I could see my best friend again. We traveled south by horseback to the new elven city of Sungrove."

My eyes widened as I heard this, but I didn't interrupt her.

"Upon entering the still developing city, it didn't take long to find Delwen."

"My—," I began to say.

"Yes, Kieran," Sylvia acknowledged. "My best friend was Delwen, your grandmother."

I was shocked that Sylvia had such a connection with my family prior to us meeting.

"We were so glad to see each other again, and she was especially glad to see me with a man," she said with a smile, remembering the old days. "Delwen obviously had news of her own, for she was pregnant with your mother."

"Your grandparents, with about 30 others from Magestice, had done a great job planning out Sungrove. The World Council had appointed Serena as the city guardian to help protect them from marauders. I could tell that she knew Ambros and I were vampires, but she kept it secret. We stayed for a month before heading back to Magestice. Delwen and Serena arranged a big going away party for us. The people of Sungrove loved a good party, and it showed," she said with a laugh. "Delwen and I hated to part ways," her tone turned sad, "but she understood why I would stay with Ambros."

"Why didn't he want to stay in Sungrove?" I asked.

"He needed to get back to his studies," she answered. "I had finished my course, but he hadn't. Also, he wanted to continue his tests on us, and

Magestice was the best place for that. Over the next few centuries, we used our illusions to appear to age normally. Delwen and I kept in touch, and we visited each other regularly. After our parents died, being the only girls in our families, we became like sisters. Serena and I also kept in touch. Whenever I would visit, she would throw a party for just the ladies. We would take that time to talk and laugh about men," she said with a little laugh. "I remember seeing you," she told me, her eyes wide with excitement.

"What? I don't remember seeing you."

"Keep in mind, I didn't look the same as I do now; I actually looked my age," she said with a grin, referring to the illusion she kept up.

"How old was I?" I asked. "I must have been young." I was amazed that not only had she known my grandmother, but she actually met me years ago.

"Oh, you were little," she explained, holding out her hand to show my size at the time. "You and Kelena wanted to be like the adults and stay out late. I remember your mother let you stay for a while, but she left the party early to put you to bed. After you and Kel hugged Delwen goodnight, and your mother left to take you home, she said that she hoped to be around to hug her great grandchildren goodnight."

She went quiet for a long moment, lost in the past. She finally spoke, but her words sounded lifeless as she stared off at nothing. "One day, as I helped her clean up after breakfast, I caught a familiar smell in the air. It was the smell of death. With all the poor animals I had drained of life since becoming a vampire, it was a smell that I had grown accustomed to. This time, however, it was coming from Delwen."

I gasped. My brain raced. Sylvia was there when she died, I thought, but I didn't speak.

"Your grandfather had gone to a spot on the mountain where he liked to meditate and pray to the Sun. I was alone with Delwen and knew that death was there to take her. 'Something's wrong,' she said to me as she reached out for something to help her maintain balance. I helped her to the floor as I began to cry tears of blood. With a look of confusion, she touched a tear from my face. I could no longer maintain the illusion. If my best friend was going to die in my arms, I was going to show her the truth. I reverted to my true form, and she was in awe that I had not physically aged for centuries. I told her that I was a vampire and that I had accepted it from Ambros."

Her speech began to waver as she remembered what happened next. "Delwen asked if I would offer it to her. I told her that we must hurry because death was already upon her. I used one of her kitchen knives to cut my neck. She began to drink as she was sure of what she wanted. As I took my first drink from her, I feared it was too late. Seconds later, I felt her heart stop beating, and she went limp in my arms. I held her, crying."

"Just then, the door opened, and your grand-father saw me holding his dead wife. 'VAMPIRE!' he yelled. 'I tried to save her,' I told him, but he had seen all that he believed he needed to see. He grabbed his elvish blade from above the mantle and charged toward me. I caught his blade between my hands. I moved one hand with lightning speed to the sword's guard for leverage and snapped the blade at the hilt. I tried to reason with him, but he continued to attack me.

I didn't want to hurt him, so I left. I ran to Serena's house to tell her what had happened. By this time, your grandfather had the townspeople gathered to destroy me. Serena trusted me to stay in her home while she left to examine Delwen's body. I focused my hearing to listen to what was being said across town. Serena used her power to recall memories from a dead mind to see the truth of what happened. She reminded the people that my death would not bring Delwen back, nor would it make the loss of her any easier. The townspeople then demanded that I be banished from Sungrove and the other elven cities forever. They argued that any elf that creates mistrust among their own race must be cast out, and being the guardian of Sungrove meant that Serena must also uphold the law. Even though I knew what my fate was to be, I awaited Serena's return."

"But you didn't kill her," I said confused that, even after proven not guilty, she was to still be punished for all time.

"Yes, but they no longer trusted me," she explained. "I had used an illusion to hide that I was a vampire, so they used that against me. When Serena returned, she not only told me of my punishment, but she told me that she was going with me. She was leaving Sungrove. She told the elves that she needed to take me to the World Council Palace and report what had happened. At the palace, Serena told the council that Sungrove needed another guardian appointed, but she wouldn't be too far away if she was ever needed. The council sent Yuri the Yellow to take her place. Serena then took me to Magestice to tell Ambros what had happened. I wasn't allowed into the city, so Serena went in my stead. She came back saying he was nowhere to be found."

"Do you think Serena knew something that she didn't tell you?" I asked, trying to make sense of it.

"I don't think so," she answered. "I couldn't venture in to check for myself, but I believe she told me the truth."

"Couldn't you have changed your form to sneak into the city?"

"With a city full of the most powerful wizards on the planet, I would have been identified immediately just for trying to hide," she explained. "The council had already sent word to all elven cities of my banishment. I couldn't risk sneaking into Magestice, so I left with Serena and stayed with her ever since."

"Wow," I told her. "Just wow. I had no idea how close you were to my family."

"When I found you in the forest, it seemed like a chance to redeem myself," she explained to me. "I was too late to save Delwen but not too late to save her grandson."

Remembering her catching me, I asked "What happened in the volcano? How did you survive?"

"I don't know," she answered. "My only guess is that Ambros passed something else onto me when he made me a vampire."

I was in awe of her beauty as she stood. The blanket that she had draped over her shoulders fell away, and she magically created a slim, black dress. It formed at her shoulders and flowed down her body.

"Does my womanly form distract you?" she asked with a smile.

To be funny, I acted startled. "What?"

She cut me a playfully sexy look. With merely a thought, she threw a blanket over my head and laughed.

I swung my arms out, sending all the blankets and pillows into the air. Everything was spinning around Sylvia. She raised her arms, and they gradually made a larger circle. I ran inside the circle and into her arms. We both laughed as we spun in the air. We locked our fingers and held our arms straight out from our sides as we continued to spin together. Sylvia and I continued to hold hands as we leaned away from each other. We spun faster and faster. We laughed harder and harder. We finally slowed down and dropped to the floor on our hands and feet. All the pillows and blankets also dropped to the floor. I jumped at her, but she dodged me. I jumped at her two more times, but she was too fast for me. She gave me a quick kiss on the nose and ran out of the room in a flash. I grabbed my breeches and chased after her. I ran out into the hall before putting them on.

A silver-haired elf in the hallway saw me. "Cover your ass!" he scolded.

I jumped into my breeches as I ran.

Sylvia turned around and ran backwards. She slowed down to let me catch up. She stayed just out of reach, giggling. She turned back around and sped up. She ran up behind five elves walking together. She passed between them as a blur of light and returned to her normal form. I did a forward flip over the elves and continued after her.

Sylvia perched herself on the railing, and golden wings sprouted from her back. She smiled at me just before flying up the center of the palace.

I ran to the railing and saw her suspended in the air several floors above me. Glass orbs, giving off a magical glow, lined the railing.

Sylvia motioned to me with her index finger to follow. I put my hands on the railing and thrust myself up and across to another railing. I sprang back and forth until I reached her. I leaped into her waiting arms, and we spun slowly in the air. She kissed me on the nose and caressed my face.

"I love you so much," she confessed, her fingers combing through my hair.

"I love you too."

We stared at each other for another moment. "Let's get you some dinner," she said to me. She quickly flew, with me still in her arms, toward the skylight above. The skylight was a magical barrier to keep out the rain. We passed through it into the night sky.

CHAPTER VII

ON THE BRINK OF WAR

The night was humid and filled with the sound of locusts. Narrow creeks reflected the moonlight as they branched out across the palace's immense flower garden. Frogs stopped croaking and hopped into the water as we walked along the stone path. The lights of the palace glittered like stars behind us.

We had been walking the palace grounds for nearly an hour, arm in arm, and she had said nothing. I sensed something was wrong. Without turning to look at her, I finally asked, "You're leaving, aren't you?" My voice sounded dead. I feared this day would come but not so soon. It had been barely a year since the destruction of Sungrove, and the loss still weighed heavily on my heart.

We stopped and faced each other. Our arms separated, but her hand found mine. Seeing tears fill her eyes gave me the answer I didn't want. "When?" I asked in the same dead tone as before.

Two tears of liquid fire streamed down her face. One tear dripped from her lip to sizzle out on the ground. The other ran under her chin. We sat on a wooden bench next to the stream.

She looked away from me as if her pain, coupled with mine, was too much to bear. "I was thinking of leaving at dawn," she answered, taking a deep breath to calm herself.

"And I cannot follow," I stated at nearly a whisper.

"I'm sorry," she apologized, touching a tear from her face to look at it. "I don't want to leave you, but I must find Ambros. I need to know what this is that I have become."

"Where will you look?"

"I haven't seen or heard from him in nearly 200 years." She turned her head toward the night sky. "I will go to the Sun."

I was shocked as I turned to face her. "So you believe he is dead? You are going to look for his spirit?"

"I need to know," she repeated.

"Once you are there, do you believe you will be able to perceive his spirit, or any others for that matter?"

Shaking her head, "I don't know that either. I know only that I need to go. I need to see with my own eyes what is there."

I understood her reason for leaving and sadly nodded my head in agreement. We both turned our gaze skyward and were quiet for a long moment.

She kissed me on the cheek and stood while still holding my hand. "I will be back. I need to tell your sister and Serena goodbye."

She pulled away from me and disappeared within the maze of bushes, trees, and plants of the palace garden. I looked back at the night sky and awaited her return.

It was nearly dawn when she returned. I had barely moved a muscle during the hour she had been gone. She sat and put her arm around me. The sky began to lighten, and birds sang to welcome the day. She kissed me on the cheek. My lips quivered, and blood tears streamed down my face, but I didn't turn away from the sky to look at her.

"This isn't goodbye," she explained. Seeing me cry upset her, and she pulled my face around to kiss me on the lips.

"Don't be gone too long," I finally said to her. I wanted to say more, but it was all I could do to get out those five simple words.

She smiled through her tears. "I won't be," she assured me. "I have to come back for you."

I closed my eyes as she kissed away my tears. She caressed my face and kissed me one last time. Then, like a streak of light, she zipped into space.

I stared out at the fading stars as the sun peeked over the horizon. My skin began to burn, but I didn't move. The blood tears that streamed down my face burned away in the sunlight. Kelena ran across the palace gardens and covered me with a thick blanket. She walked me back to the palace.

The dragon lords were having another meeting in the council chamber. Serena, Kel, and I had been asked to join them. The waiters made their way around the table to take up dishes and refill glasses. The council had been in session for more than two hours, and we seemed farther away now from agreeing on a plan of action than when we started.

"If we do nothing," Ariana said directly to Ian, "and we continue to rule as we have always done, a war of the races will overwhelm us."

"Ariana is right," Drakuss added before Ian had time to speak. "Magnus' course of action may seem extreme, but it will save us from hundreds of years of war."

"Listen to what you are saying," Ian said to everyone, not believing that his own council was suggesting they follow Magnus. "You are proposing we, the World Council, who are among the oldest and wisest beings on the planet, rise up and destroy the ones that we have sworn to our forefathers to protect."

"Don't you see?" Kildren asked. "We are faced with a problem that—"

"A problem that will work itself out," Mya cut him off. "We—"

"But at what cost?" Kildren cut back. "War is coming," he stated strongly to Mya. He then looked at everyone at the council table. "We can kill thousands now to save millions later."

The council chamber's double doors opened and Magnus entered the room. Everyone stood. Once again, Magnus motioned nonchalantly for us to sit.

"Please, there's no reason to stand," he said with a smile, but no one sat.

"Why are you here?" Ian asked, obviously not happy to see him.

Magnus walked over to one of the windows and looked out at the cloudy sky. "You know why I have come," he said with his back to the council, "to find out who is with me and who isn't." The tone of his voice reflected confidence.

"We will not banish you as the council did before us," Gwyneth spoke out with a threatening tone.

Magnus walked over and took a seat at the table next to Drakuss.

Everyone but Ian sat down. "That was your warning," Ian added with a stare that burned to the bone. "We will destroy you if you continue with this."

Magnus met his stare, and the tension in the room began to build.

I was suddenly afraid. Kel and I sat amongst the most powerful creatures on the planet, and it felt as if, at any moment, the room could explode in a fiery inferno. No one moved in fear that it would trigger a war right here in the council chamber. Few, if any, would survive at this range. I felt Kelena's hand close over mine that I had rested on my lap.

"Even if the threat against humans is taken care of, why do you insist that the magical creatures hide from them?" Ariana asked Magnus with a calm, soothing voice to break the stare and dispel the tension in the room.

Ian took a deep breath to calm himself and he slowly returned to his seat.

"Time is almost at a standstill," Magnus

explained. "Life has been the same for millennia. Since most humans are incapable of spell casting, they are forced to think of new ways to do things. If the humans didn't have to worry about defending their cities from goblins or ogres, they would create things to make their lives better."

"Why should we care how the humans live their lives?" Mya the Green Dragon Lord asked.

"Since the magical creatures live such long lives," Magnus continued, "they have fewer than five offspring within an 800-year period. The humans, on the other hand, have about seven children within a 20-year period. The humans will populate the world much quicker than we will."

"What is your point, Magnus?" Ian asked sharply.

"My point is the humans will be doing all the work," Magnus answered through a big grin as if he had solved some ancient mystery. "They will be making advancements that we all can benefit from."

Everyone was quiet for a moment as they envisioned a peaceful world.

"Yes, your plan is well conceived," Ian finally admitted. "But if your inevitable outcome is to occur, then it will have to occur on its own," his tone changed. With his answer for the world's growing problems, Magnus had gained a bit of respect with Ian.

I noticed Ariana, Drakuss, and Kildren looked at Ian in disapproval. The others kept their eyes on Magnus.

Magnus shook his head as he stood, knowing that he had said all he could say.

"I am the senior member of the World

Council," Ian added. "My orders are to be obeyed." His strict tone of authority came through again, and with a drop of his fist on the table, Ian announced firmly, "We will not speed the advancement of human civilization by the killing of innocent beings. We will continue to rule as we have for millennia."

Magnus matched his unwavering tone, "This will happen, Ian, with or without your approval." He began to leave.

"If you oppose us, you will be destroyed!" Ian's strong words rang out as Magnus left the room.

No one said a word. Ian stared at the table, rubbing his troubled brow. He then looked around the table to each individual. Everyone waited patiently for Ian to speak, to voice an answer that would solve the world's problems, but he didn't. Instead, he dismissed us with the wave of his hand.

I was looking out the window at the night sky when Kelena entered my room. Without turning around to look at her, I asked, "Will you come with me if I leave?"

"Of course; I cannot live without you," she said, putting her arms around me and laying her head on my shoulder.

I smelled a fresh kill emanating from her. I sometimes forgot that my sister was a werewolf. My senses told me she caught a young buck. The smell was intoxicating, reminding me that I needed to feed.

"So where are we going?" she asked excitedly as she jumped around in front of me, her wanderlust shining brightly in her eyes.

I couldn't help smiling. "I was thinking we could move to Magestice as we had planned."

"Yeah, let's go! The people here are a little too sour for my taste anyway," she added with a sly grin. She gave me a quick kiss on the forehead and ran for the door. "It won't take me long to get ready," she said just before leaving the room.

I walked over and looked at myself for a moment in the mirror. I took a deep breath to relax. Was I making the right decision to leave? My parents were murdered. My home was destroyed. The ones that orchestrated the attack were still out there. Because I wasn't a dragon, I could not be on the World Council, but I could help them try to maintain peace. What Magnus said did make sense. 'If you already know the inevitable outcome, why not help it along?' I also saw Ian's point of view that we couldn't go to war to annihilate a number of races simply because we had a vision. With the council seemingly split on the decision, it only made me worry more that we were teetering on the brink of war.

I walked to the door and looked out into the hall. Just outside the door, on the left, were two wicker baskets. I looked in one to find a small stack of clean clothes and a pair of sandals. I took them into my room. I placed the clean clothes on a small table as I undressed. I took my shirt off and held it up to examine. It was ragged and dirty. I dropped the dirty clothes on the floor. Once I finished undressing, I put my right hand out, and moisture was drawn from the air to form a vertical puddle of water. It looked like a big oval piece of shimmering glass suspended in the air. Once the puddle was big enough, I stepped through it. I was not wet, but I looked perfectly clean. The water had stayed within its puddle but now looked dingy. The water then fell to the floor and quickly evaporated, leaving behind the dirt. I swept the dirt outside and off the balcony. I put the clean clothes on, including a robe that was in the stack, and tied on the pair of sandals. I picked up my pile of dirty clothes and looked around the room one last time before I left. Everything looked neat and clean. Once I stepped out, the magical orb that lit the room went dark, and I dropped my dirty clothes in the second basket that sat outside the room.

I walked to Serena's room, which was three doors up from mine. I opened the door and saw her standing out on the balcony. I walked out to join her.

"Hi," she said, glancing at me. "Kelena told me the two of you are leaving."

"We are going to attend the Temple of High Magic in Magestice."

"Why would you want to attend a school to learn magic when you can attain all the knowledge that you can possibly want right here?" she asked me. "The council has a vast library and . . . and you're a vampire. I'm sure you can find someone here willing to let you feed on them, so you can learn a new spell or skill."

"I believe it to be impolite to invade the minds of others."

"It's not considered an invasion if you are welcomed," she said with a smile.

I returned the smile as I began to have second thoughts again of leaving, but I quickly remembered my original plan to live and study in Magestice. "If I learn everything instantly, how will I spend the rest of eternity? Forever is an awfully long time to have nothing to do."

"I'm sorry." Serena's smile turned sad. "I'm just trying to keep you here . . . keep you close," she added with loneliness in her eyes.

I held her gaze for a moment before asking, "Why don't you come with us?"

She placed her hands on the balcony railing as she looked out over the moonlit palace gardens. "I have been thinking of staying here and working for the council. Right now, Ian can use anyone willing to help."

With a teasing smile, I asked, "Well, if you happen to find some free time between babysitting ogres and helping old goblins cross the trail, will you come visit me?"

Serena burst with laughter! "It seems you have a sense of humor after all. I was actually starting to worry. And of course I will come visit you," she said with a sincere smile. "You are my best friend," she added, hugging me. "It will be good for you to get out, and busy yourself to take your mind off Sylvia."

I looked out at the countless stars. "Do you think she will return?" my voice stained with fear and doubt.

"She will," Serena answered confidently, draping an arm over my shoulders. She too turned her attention to the stars. "She just needs time."

I put my arm around her waist. "I hate to leave, but I do need to get away for a while. Maybe Kel and I will work for the council once we finish our schooling."

Serena pulled away with a bit of excitement. "The three of us can work together!" We both smiled at the thought, and she gave me a kiss on the cheek. "Would you like to drink from me before you leave?"

The question caught me off guard for a moment, but only for a moment. "Yes."

I pushed thick, red curls away from her neck and sank my teeth in. I drank slowly from her, savoring the taste. Her heartbeat stayed steady and calm. After a long drink, I released her. I rubbed my cheek against hers and gave her a kiss before whispering, "My beautiful friend, oh, how I wish I could give you life everlasting."

Serena was teary-eyed. "I am honored that you would present me with the gift of eternal life. I wish my body could accept it, but it would take more blood than you can give. I will grow old and pass into oblivion."

"I'm sorry," I told her, lowering my head.

"Don't be," she said, lifting my chin. "Not everyone can live forever. If so, the world would be overpopulated."

"I don't want everyone to be immortal, just the ones that I love," I told her on the brink of tears.

She gave me a loving smile that turned sad. "I'm going to miss you, Kieran of Sungrove."

Her words brought a smile to my face. We stood quietly together, looking out at the stars.

CHAPTER VIII

TO MAGESTICE

Serena led me and Kel to a room and knocked twice on the door. We heard, "Yes?" from inside, and the doors opened. There were beautiful paintings on the walls and shelves holding wonderfully shaped vases made from clay and glass. One of the green-haired elves was molding marble as if it were wet clay. The tips of his fingers were glowing with a white light as he pressed into his project. It appeared that the finished sculpture would be a female elf with wild hair. Dust, dirt, and chunks of stone littered the floor. He paused from his work, wiping his hands off with a towel. "Hi Serena. What can I do for ya?"

Serena introduced us to him. "Sonido, this is Kieran and Kelena."

"Good evening," he greeted us with a bow.

"They would like to go to Magestice," Serena

told him. "I was wondering if you had time to take them?"

"Oh yeah! Oh yeah! I can take them," he answered. "No problem. I can even grab a few supplies while I'm there."

"Great," Serena answered with a chuckle at Sonido's exuberance. She turned back to us and sighed heavily. "Well, it looks like this is it."

"No, it's not. We will just have to visit one another," Kelena told her.

Serena smiled. "Yes, we will. We will visit one another." She gave Kelena a hug goodbye. "I'll see you soon." She gave her a kiss on the forehead and then stepped over to me. "I'm going to stay to find out how I can help the council, and I will come visit in a few weeks."

"I can't wait until your visit. We're going to have so much fun," I told her.

"I'm sure I'll be bored out of my mind with you two gone. When I go to see you, I may not want to come back," she laughed.

"That will be okay," I said as I felt her melt in my arms. We held each other for a moment, and she touched her nose to mine before pulling away slowly.

"I love you, Kieran. I love you both," she told us as she backed away.

"And we love you," Kel and I said in unison.

Sonido stood between us and draped his arms over mine and Kelena's shoulders. "Are we ready to go?" he asked with a bit too much excitement in Kelena's face.

"I think so," Kelena answered nervously.

Serena and I laughed as a flash of bright light

exploded from Sonido, enveloping us.

"Hmm, that's strange," I heard Sonido say. The light faded away, and the three of us were standing in the middle of a dirt road cut through a dense forest. The morning sun broke through the trees to light our path. I quickly pulled my hood up and drew my hands into the long sleeves of my cloak to avoid getting burned.

"Where are we? Where did you take us?" Kelena asked him.

"There seems to be some kind of magical barrier over Magestice," he explained. "We were blocked from teleporting into the city, so I brought us as close as I could get."

"How far away are we?" Kelena asked him in a stern tone since we could see nothing in either direction.

He swallowed hard, giving away his nervousness, as he didn't wish to make my sister angry. "Um, a few miles," he told her, forcing a smile through his fear.

She loved that he was afraid of her. "Well, we better start walking. Lead the way," she told him. Without another word, he did as he was told.

I felt Kel's hand reach for mine as we walked quietly down the path. I extended my fingers a bit, so she could take hold of them. I didn't have to concentrate to read her thoughts. I saw them instantly and with more clarity than ever before. I saw myself through her eyes, at that very moment, as we walked together. She imagined Tess sitting on my shoulder, hitching a ride through the forest. I squeezed Kel's hand tighter and turned to face her. "I miss her too."

With that said, I could see by the blankness on her face that she didn't know I was in her thoughts. Just as I registered her expression, she began to cry. I led her to the edge of the forest, and we sat down on tree roots that were exposed from the ground.

Sonido didn't walk much farther before noticing we had stopped. He gave us some privacy for a moment.

"It doesn't seem right, her not being with us," Kelena said to me, choked up from the tears.

"Nothing seems right anymore," I corrected her with my own tears filling my eyes. I noticed that she didn't cry tears of blood. Her tears were as they should be.

She seemed confused for a moment when she saw mine. I rubbed a tear from my eye and offered it for her to examine more closely. She leaned forward and sniffed it. "You're right," she agreed with a raised brow. "Nothing seems right anymore." She wiped the tears from her face and stood, pulling me to my feet.

With Sonido several yards ahead of us, we continued on the path to Magestice.

"If the dragons are so powerful," I began, "why can't they read Magnus' mind to know his intentions without having to waste time in council meetings?"

"I asked Serena the same question," Kel answered, finding it a coincidence. "She said that Magnus is very powerful and can block their telepathy, but even if they could, by council law, they can't enter another being's mind without invitation."

"What?" I exclaimed in disbelief.

With a shrug of her shoulders, "I know," she agreed with me. "I don't understand either. If I had the power to save the world, I would," she expressed.

I turned to her and asked, "Are you saying you would follow Magnus?" I was more curious than shocked at her statement.

"Well," she began to answer but paused to arrange her thoughts, "he does make a good argument. I mean, populations are growing. We may not see it where we are right now, but the races fight over land, and it will continue until one race dominates." She then gave me a sly grin. "Are you saying you would side with Ian?"

"I'm not sure," I answered. "But, like you said, Magnus makes a valid argument. I just don't understand why the world's races can't peacefully coexist. Do they not see that they can accomplish so much more by working together?"

Kelena didn't have an answer for me.

The farther we went, the darker the sky became. It was as if we were walking straight into a massive storm.

"Looks like we may get wet, brother."

"At least we will be out of the sun," I told her, removing my hood and tying my hair back with a brown ribbon. "What is that?" I asked, squinting my eyes, looking far ahead of us.

Sonido, hearing my question, answered, "It's an elf."

"He is approaching fast," Kelena added.

The three of us stepped aside to let him by. Kelena moved left. Sonido and I moved right. The elf zipped by with super speed, leaving us in the dust.

"I wonder what that was about," Kelena said, fanning the dust from her face.

"I don't know." I spotted another runner heading our way. "Maybe you should ask this one."

She turned and barely had time enough to say, "Why are you . . ." and the second running elf was gone. "He didn't even slow down!" she exclaimed.

I stood across the trail from her, cracking up with laughter. Even Sonido chuckled a little.

"It's not funny!" she scolded but with a smile creeping across her face. "Wait," she said, seeing several speeding elves in a row. "I'm about to have another chance." Her face beamed with excitement as four elves approached. "Why are you . . . ? Is the storm . . . ? Did someone . . . ? Please stop. STOP!"

All four elves zipped by us, paying no attention to my frustrated sister.

I stood, with my hands on my knees, laughing at her. Sonido tried to hold back his laughter with both hands over his mouth. Kelena was mad, but we couldn't help laughing at her standing there in a cloud of dust.

I saw the wolf in her eyes. She lifted her arms from her sides, closed her eyes, and took a deep, relaxing breath. She opened her eyes, and I saw that the wolf was gone.

I took her hand in mine. "Looks like we'll just have to see what's going on for ourselves."

The three of us quickened our pace toward Magestice.

We reached Magestice but found that it was under attack! Several fire breathing dragons were flying over, incinerating the city. There were vampires there too. Some were collecting precious metals, gems, weapons, and books, loading them onto wagons. The storm clouds must have been created to block the sunlight, so they could assist in the raid.

Being unable to teleport to safety, Sonido turned and ran.

"They are destroying Magestice as they did Sungrove," Kelena cried out.

"Yes, but it appears they are only killing those who fight back," I told her. "The elves that flee are spared."

"Let's see if we can help these people escape the city. But we must be careful; I sense werewolves here," Kelena warned before we ran in.

People were running in all directions to escape the attack. Families were carrying their children to safety. Others were carrying only the bare necessities.

Kel and I looked around to see where our help was needed, and I noticed that none of the city's spellcasters were trying to defend the city. Magestice was the epicenter for the arcane arts. I found it odd that there was no one using magic against the city's attackers. I saw an elf running with a spell book under his arm, so I grabbed him. "Why isn't anyone using magic against them?"

"Nothing works! There must be a very powerful caster among them to cut us off like this!" he answered.

I looked up at the circling dragons for just a moment before turning back to see the elf leaving the city.

Kelena's head turned to focus her hearing on something. "Someone needs our help!" she yelled before running through the city. I followed her into a burning building to find a woman trying to free her husband from a large wooden support beam that had fallen on him. Kelena gripped the support beam, and her muscles grew to give her the strength to lift it. I helped the woman get her husband out of the building. Kelena followed us out.

"Thank you," the man said to us.

"Yes, thank you," his wife repeated, coughing from inhaling too much smoke.

"You are very welcome," Kelena told them. "We're glad we could help."

"You both will be fine," I told them, "but you should see a healer once you escape the city."

"We will," the woman assured us. "Thank you again." With her husband's arm over her shoulder, she helped him walk, and they headed toward the forest.

I told Kelena, "They would have died if it were not for your keen sense of hearing to locate them. That woman would not have left her husband's side to save herself."

She continued to watch the couple leave the city. "I wonder if that's how our parents died—huddled together under a collapsing roof, or did they make a last stand against Sungrove's attackers?"

I placed a comforting hand on her shoulder. "I don't know, but we don't have time to think about that right now. Let's see if we can use our powers to save what's left of this city."

She turned back to me wearing the slightest of smiles. "Yes, and then maybe we can save the world," she added. "Where to now?"

It looked like every building was burning, but

standing tall among them, the city's center spire remained suspiciously untouched. Kel and I looked at each other, but we didn't have to say a word; we knew the Magestice Temple of High Magic was where we should go.

As we made our way through the city, we saw the homes and buildings being ransacked. The looters paid us little attention as they could smell that we were immortals like them. Some were vampires. The others must have been werewolves but in their elf forms.

We no longer saw dragons circling the skies, but the closer we got to the temple, the more we saw charred corpses littering the blackened streets. It was as if a dragon flew over and killed dozens with one breath. The smell of burnt flesh was unbearable. We covered our nose and mouth with our sleeve.

We reached the temple and stood frozen at the sight of it. Bodies were lying over top of one another!

"This must be where the city's first and last line of defense stood their ground," I told Kelena with my voice muffled from my sleeve.

Most of the bodies were burnt to a crisp. Some were butchered, ripped to shreds, perhaps by werewolves. Some of them looked like they were crushed, and others even looked partially liquefied! What a grisly sight it was.

"It looks like, when they realized a powerful Dispel Magic was cast upon them, they had to resort to using swords and bows," I told her.

"Without magic, they didn't stand a chance," she added. "These people were slaughtered."

"These people tried to stop us from completing our mission," a voice came from behind, startling us.

We turned quickly to find the vampire Dirk perched atop the rubble of a collapsed building.

"And what would that be?" Kelena questioned him angrily.

"To wipe this city from existence," he replied arrogantly.

"Then where is Magnus?" I asked him. "He is the one behind all this, is he not?"

"Oh, he's inside," Dirk answered with a nod toward the temple, "with Artimes and the others."

"The others?" I asked.

"Yes," he answered with a grin. "It's amazing the loyalty one gains when eternal life is offered as reward." His eyes never left us as he stood and made his way down the rubble. He carried no weapon but wore lightweight leather armor that left his legs and arms free to move.

"You can't mean you bribed them to turn against their home?" Kelena asked in disbelief.

"That's exactly what I mean," Dirk answered as he stepped down from the last chunk of broken stone.

We heard the doors unlock, and Dirk looked past us to the temple. Kel and I turned to see the doors open, pushing bodies aside, and Artimes step out. The elder vampire wasn't wearing armor but was dressed in the finest of clothing. He paused to take in the scene. The thick, dark clouds and black smoke blocked out the sun. Every home and building had been destroyed. Fires still burned, and their flames reached high into the sky. The look on Artimes' face was that of triumph.

With the dead littering the temple steps and the

surrounding area, he would have to step on the bodies to make his way down to us, but he didn't. Instead, he pressed the palms of his hands together. He then separated them, and with that simple gesture, the dead that lie before him divided to clear a path.

"So the young immortal siblings have come to give up their immortality," Artimes stated with a laugh as he walked down the temple steps.

"You will not be so lucky to escape, this time," Dirk added with a more serious tone.

Kelena, with her eyes tearing up, remembered home. "Why are you doing this?" she screamed out.

"We cannot let the magical creatures be discovered by humans," Artimes explained smoothly. "The humans are too young a race to be introduced to magic."

"So you are going to destroy all the magical beings?" I asked, doing my best to stay calm and focused so that my feelings didn't distract me from the danger Dirk and Artimes posed.

"We are going to destroy the ones who cannot or will not keep their true identities secret," Artimes answered with a more irritated tone. "So are you with us?" he asked.

Both Kel and I answered, "No," in unison.

"I thought not," he said with a bloodthirsty grin. He leaped at me, kicking me in the chin, knocking me back.

I regained my balance and went on the offensive.

Kelena began to change into her wolf form. Dirk ran at her, hoping to get in some free hits, but she fought back as she was changing. The only hits that he landed only seemed to enrage her. He noticed her increasing speed and strength with each passing second as Kelena began to deflect his every attack. Dirk was finally knocked to the ground as he watched Kelena fully transform into a werewolf and howl with anticipation of killing him.

Dirk quickly got to his feet and stood ready for battle. Kelena charged him, but he back flipped to the top of the rubble pile. Two 1' ethereal blades extended from each of his fists. Just as she leaped after him, he jumped to attack her in the air. She caught his wrists and slung him away. He hit hard on the ground.

Artimes and I continued to fight, but he seemed to be holding back, savoring it. Every kick was blocked, every punch deflected. He only struck to anger me, pressing me to hasten my attacks so that I would tire. I needed to get the upper hand before I became too weak to win this battle. I threw a left haymaker, but he stepped back causing me to miss. I used the haymaker as a diversion to buy time to summon an ethereal blade with my right hand. I thrust the blade at his neck, but he was always a step ahead of me. He forced my blade down with one of his own. He stepped forward, headbutting me on the bridge of my nose. I stumbled back, stunned, but he didn't take this chance to end it. With a smile, he said, "Oh, I'm not finished with you just yet."

Kelena charged down the rubble toward Dirk as he lay face down on the ground. He rolled over in time to swing at her, slicing her left arm and the right side of her face. He jumped to his feet. He swung at her again, but she caught it and ripped his arm from the shoulder. Dirk screamed in pain, and with his loss of concentration, his ethereal blades vanished. He gripped his bleeding shoulder and dropped to one knee as Kelena threw his left arm to the ground. Sure that she had defeated him, Kelena proudly made her way toward him to deliver the killing blow.

Dirk waited until the last second, then created a 6" ethereal katar and uppercut under her rib cage into her chest. "Now you die," he said victoriously. He ripped the heart from her chest, and she fell backwards to the ground.

Both Artimes and I saw her fall. I quickly scrambled to her, but there was nothing I could do. I held her head as she changed back to her true form. Her body was dead, but I could feel her thoughts! She was fighting for life! Her mind reached frantically out to me, so I let her enter my thoughts to know the love I felt for her and then nothing. I pulled her face close to mine and cried, "Kel? Kel? Kelena! Come back. Please come back, Kel."

Magnus stepped out of the temple's open doors. He looked down at us from atop the steps. Dragon wings sprouted from his back, and he took to the air.

"Now it is your turn," Artimes said to me with a smile. "Let us finish this."

My face was stained with blood tears from crying over the death of my sister. I looked up at Dirk and Artimes with hatred in my eyes. I blinked and time seemed to slow down.

Artimes bit his tongue and flicked the blood to taunt me.

I took a deep breath to calm myself, and time returned to normal speed. I took off my cloak to cover my sister's naked body. I kissed her forehead and stood to face Artimes and Dirk.

"No. Leave him. It's finished," Magnus' voice boomed out. He had taken the form of a Red Dragon. Artimes, Dirk, and I shielded our eyes from the dirt and debris that was blown from the force of his wings as he landed, crushing the dead beneath his feet.

Dirk, still holding Kelena's heart, turned away from me, but Artimes paid no attention to Magnus' order. He began to circle me like a lion closing in on his prey.

Magnus spoke again. "We have done what we came to do. Now let's go."

Artimes ignored his orders. He leaped at me, but Magnus snatched him in his hand. He brought Artimes up close, breathed in deep, and burned him to dust with a long, fiery breath.

Magnus then turned to Dirk. He took hold of him carefully and leaped into the sky. He outstretched his wings to gain altitude and flew away from Magestice.

I ran back to Kelena. I knelt down, pulled her body up close, and cried as the city burned around me.

I finally decided to carry my sister's body to our place on the mountain where we used to watch the sunset and release her spirit. I wrapped her body in strips of cloth torn from the clothing of the many dead elves. As I carried her body through Magestice, I saw Magnus' servants still at work dismantling the city and filling wagons with things they wished to keep. I saw a wooden sign burning on the ground that read Ilithor's Craft Shop, and I remembered the marble statue that Sonido was working on. This must be where he planned to get supplies.

I reached the edge of the forest and found horses tied there. I took one and carried Kelena's body south toward Sungrove.

Day and night, I rode. I stayed in the shadows of trees during the day and fed on rabbits and deer to keep me healthy.

I reached Sungrove, but there was nothing left. There was no order of stacked stones to show where houses once stood. There were no flower beds. There was nothing lying around to show that anyone was ever here. "This place has been cleaned," I said aloud, looking over the area. "The trees have grown tall. I have lost track of time. The forest has reclaimed Sungrove. Can it be that a century has passed since Sungrove's destruction?"

I left the horse at the foot of the mountain and carried Kelena to the top. The trail to the mountain top had long since grown up in weeds and shrubs. With a ball of light in my hand and her completely wrapped body draped over my shoulder, I made my way to the spot where we used to watch the sunset together. Unlike the path here, our spot appeared the same. I carefully placed her body on the ground and sat next to her.

With a heavy sigh and a heavy heart, I spoke to her, hoping she could hear me. "Hi Kel. I'm sorry I couldn't save you. I'm so sorry." My lips quivered, and my eyes bled. I wiped away the tears and looked at my stained fingers. "This blood coursing through my veins may keep me alive indefinitely, but my strength left with you. You are the other half that makes me whole. I became a vampire so that I could save you, but I failed. I failed you. Dirk took away our home. He took away our friends. He took away our family. And now he has taken you." I paused, thinking for a moment. "Dirk took your heart. Sylvia said that the only way to kill a werewolf was by silver or destroying the heart. I can't send you to the Sun yet. I have to save you, and I believe there is still a chance."

I carried Kelena's body back down the mountain and draped her over the horse. I rode on to Sylvia and Serena's underground home. I used my magic to clear the entrance and carried Kelena's body inside. The floor felt damp under my feet, and the air was dank. My night vision cut through the dark as I made my way down the hallway to the main room. Tree roots had broken through the stone walls to allow moisture in.

"It shouldn't take me long to get this place cleaned up like it once was, but first I need to take care of you," I said to my sister, who I was still holding in my arms. I held her wrapped body above the wet floor. I magically drew the water up and used it to freeze her body. I pulled my hands away just as she froze in a block of ice. I returned to the surface and sealed the place before riding the horse back to Magestice.

I made it back to the city and saw that it was still being cleaned like Sungrove was perhaps a century ago. Only a few bonfires lit the city. The blocks used for building was being magically broken down to dust. Even the Temple of High Magic was quickly being worn away.

I dismounted my horse and approached one of the elves working to clear an area. I didn't have to see his fangs to tell that he was a vampire; I could sense it.

He turned to acknowledge my presence. "I'm looking for some marble," I told him. "Have you seen any?"

He pointed a finger. "There are a few wagons designated for carrying only marble. They should be on the western side of the city."

"Thank you," I told him, bowing my head slightly.

"You're welcome," he said, returning to his duties.

I got on my horse and rode over to find two wagons loaded down with marble that was collected from the city. One had unused blocks, and the other had broken statues and pedestals. I tied my stolen horse to one wagon. I took three more horses that were tied nearby and got the wagons ready to go.

Another elf vampire noticed that I was about to leave and yelled out at me. "You there."

I looked at him but, afraid that I had been caught, didn't say a word.

"We'll have another couple of loads for you to take to Ostrava, when you return," he told me.

"Yes sir," I responded to not raise suspicion.

"And don't let them see your ears!" he added.

I gave him a smile and nodded as he went about his business. I stood between the two horses that will be pulling the second wagon and whispered elvish magic in their ears to follow closely. I got on the first wagon and took the southern trail out of the city. If Ostrava was to the west, no one noticed me going the wrong direction.

The journey was slower this time, but I made it back without a problem. I carried all the marble into one of the underground rooms. Kel's ice had not melted very much, but I added more to it anyway before heading back to Magestice for more marble. I thought I should take all that I could get because I may want it sometime between then and eternity.

I returned to Magestice a few nights later, and just as the elf vampire had said, there were indeed two more wagons loaded with marble. As I tied the horses to the other wagons, another vampire rode up pulling a wagon.

"Do you know where we are supposed to take these wagons?" he asked me.

I then noticed that he was not an elf but a human. "I'm taking these wagons south," I told him, hoping he would leave this task with me alone.

"Great!" he said excitedly. "I'm tired of dusting rocks. I need to get away for a couple of days."

I laughed at his comment about dusting rocks and thought that I should play along for now. Perhaps I could get some information out of him along the way. "You can sit with me on the lead wagon, if you want," I told him.

The human looked at me strangely and asked, "Won't you need me to follow you on this wagon?"

"No. No, that's not necessary. I'll just tell them to follow us," I answered him with a grin.

He climbed down from his wagon as I whispered in the horses' ears. "You elves know some handy tricks," he told me in amazement.

We climbed up on the lead wagon and began the journey south.

"My name is Sebastian," he said, extending his hand. "What's yours?"

I looked down at his hand, wondering what he

was doing. It was almost like the peaceful greeting but different. It was only one hand, and it was turned on its side. I slowly extended my hand in the same manner, and he took hold of it. He gave it a little shake and let go. "Um, my name is Kieran," I told him, still a little confused.

"Nice to meet you, Kieran," he said with a big smile. "So how long have you been a vampire?"

I thought for a moment, looking down the dark trail ahead of us. "I'm not sure," I answered. "I've lost track of time. What year is it?"

Sebastian laughed at me. "Wow! You really have lost track of time. It is the year 540."

Five-forty, I thought. I wasn't off by much. "Ninety-one years," I answered him. "Time goes by so quickly."

"I was turned a year ago today," he told me. "Would today be called my black birthday?"

I didn't look at him. I only shrugged my shoulders. Maybe it wasn't such a good idea to let him come along.

"Well anyway, this girl bit my friend, and then he gave it to me. I lost my job because my boss caught me biting a customer. He told me I was a devil. I didn't hear the girl complaining. HAHAAHAAA!"

My hands began to shake. I could barely crack a fake smile. This kid wouldn't shut up!

"My real birthday is in three months and eleven days," he continued. "I will be 20."

I could feel the rage boiling up inside me. He knew nothing.

"I think my daddy is going to buy me another horse!"

I grabbed his head with both hands and gave it a good twist. "Happy birthday," I told him as his body fell over on the seat. "I don't know if that is enough to kill a vampire, but at least you are quiet."

I took a moment to calm down. "I'm sorry. It's just that your constant chatter was driving me mad!" I grabbed hold of his shirt and sat him up straight. His head fell unnaturally back, but his blank stare fell on me.

"I don't know why, but since my sister was . . . taken from me, I've felt different. I know feeling different is natural when someone close to you dies, but I feel on the brink of exploding." I paused for a moment, remembering me and my sister growing up. She always pushed herself to be just a little faster than me, just a little stronger. "Kelena and I were twins, see?" I began to explain. I looked over at Sebastian's dead face. "Well, I guess you don't." I stared off again, remembering how life used to be. "Oh, how I wish I were back at the dinner table, talking over a meal with my family," I whispered. I snapped back to the present, still riding a wagon down a long, dark road. I looked over at poor, dead Sebastian and smiled. "I suppose you do too," I told him with a laugh.

Just then, I heard him draw breath! He was not dead! It seemed a broken neck wasn't enough to kill a vampire. It only stuns us for a short while. I listened closely and heard a faint heartbeat slowly working its dark magic to revive him.

"I am sorry Sebastian, but I cannot let you live. I will not be feeding from you either; I don't think I can stand having your blood coursing through my veins," I told him in disgust. "Now how can I get rid of you?" I asked aloud, more to myself than to him.

I remembered my lessons with Yuri when we had to magically melt away our ice sculptures. I placed my hand on Sebastian's shoulder and concentrated on creating a sphere of light within him. It grew brighter and hotter as it quickly burned him to ashes, and the wind blew them away.

I traveled the rest of the way to the underground sanctuary in silence. The horses pulling the other two wagons followed me as they should.

As I unloaded the marble from the wagons, I found that the one Sebastian was originally riding wasn't loaded with marble. It was loaded with gold, silver, and precious stones! "Thank you, Sebastian. I wonder if these three loads were collected from the temple. No matter, I have work to do."

As I took everything underground, I saw that Kelena's ice was still holding. I went back to the surface and ordered the horses to return to Magestice without me. I hoped everyone will be too busy to notice three wagons returning with no drivers.

With a heavy sigh, I walked down into the dark and closed the entrance behind me.

CHAPTER IX

PRESERVED IN STONE

As I pressed my fingers in the marble, molding it to my liking, I heard the stone slab covering the entrance being moved. I paused, listening for any sign of who may be entering. I then heard the doors open.

"Kieran?" a familiar voice called for me. "Kelena?"

It was Serena! "I'm here," I answered and ran through the dark toward the entrance.

She caught me in her arms. "When news of Magestice reached the palace, I had to come look for you," she said, relieved to see me. "With nowhere else to go, if you survived, I knew you would come here."

From the expression on my face, she could see that something was terribly wrong. "What's wrong? Where is Kelena?" she asked, looking past me down the long, dark passageway.

I opened my mouth but no words escaped. I couldn't speak. Visions of my sister, lifeless in my arms, overwhelmed me, and I collapsed, crying in Serena's arms.

"Oh no. Oh no," she said through gasping breaths as she held me. She then helped me down the stairs. She magically illuminated her old home and took me to the main room. She saw the marble statue that I had been working on. It was a life-size statue of me and Kelena sitting, leaned back, and gazing off into the distance. Tess was sitting on my shoulder.

I sat on the edge of the empty pool in the center of the room as Serena quietly sobbed. "Dirk killed her," I finally said. "He took her heart."

Serena didn't say anything. She only looked at me, shaking her head. She couldn't believe what she was hearing.

"If I can get her heart, I may be able to bring her back," I told her with a glimmer of hope in my eyes.

Hesitantly, Serena told me, "She's gone, Kieran. She's gone."

"No!" I yelled. I walked over to the statue. "I won't accept it."

She stood behind me, placing a consoling hand on my back. "Even if you did, somehow bring her back to life, her memories will be gone. They only last a short while before fading away. She would be like a newborn child living a different life to become a different person. Your sister is dead."

I walked away from her. Not wanting to accept it, I tried to change the subject. "Did Sonido bring word of the attack to the council?"

"No, he never returned. The council received word from the lucky few that escaped the massacre."

"What?" I asked, shocked by her answer. "Sonido never returned?"

"So you don't know what happened to him?" she asked.

"No. When we arrived at Magestice and saw that it was under attack, he ran."

"He ran?" she repeated. "Why didn't he teleport the three of you back to the palace?"

"There was a very powerful Dispel Magic cast over the entire city during the attack," I explained to her. "We couldn't port into the city, so Sonido took us as close as he could. We then made the rest of the journey on foot. Kelena sensed other werewolves in the area. Perhaps Sonido was caught shortly after leaving us."

"He left you?" Serena asked surprised.

"Yes," I answered. "But Kel and I could have followed him. Maybe we should have followed him," I added. "Instead, we continued into the city, not to defend it but to help people escape."

"And did you?" she asked optimistically.

"Yes," I answered with a smile. "Kelena saved a loving couple from a fire."

She smiled. "Good." Her smile turned sad as she asked me, "Did you happen to learn who was behind the attack?"

"We learned that an undetermined number of wizards were offered immortality for their allegiance to Magnus. It was their combined powers that weakened the city."

"Magnus," she repeated through gritted teeth.

"We suspected him but had no confirmation. We must tell the council immediately. Are you ready to go back with me?"

I looked back at my sculpture, which I was near to completing. "Yes, I think so."

She took hold of my hand. "Then we must hurry," she said, leading me to the surface. She closed the doors and pushed the rock over them. She gave me a firm embrace as leathery wings sprouted from her back, and she carried us into the air.

CHAPTER X

WAR HAS COME

I sat alone in an immense library, finishing a book. The library filled two levels of the World Council Palace. It was very relaxing to hear the heavy rain outside that afternoon.

I looked over at the empty chair next to me and imagined Kelena sitting there with a book, her legs draped over the arm. She gave me a smile before continuing with her reading. I blinked, and she was gone. I was once again alone in the library. I sighed heavily and walked over to put my book in its rightful place on the shelf. There were hundreds of books before it, and there were still hundreds more ahead; enough to keep me busy for quite some time. There were books about the history of each race of beings, wars and conflicts written in detail, journals of the previous World Council members, and tomes of magic.

There were also wonderful works of fiction, written to inspire and entertain.

The book that I just finished reading was the journal of Assim, Ariana's grandfather. He served as head of the council a millennium ago. It seemed he kept a fairly detailed account of his life, so I found it strange that entire months seemed purposely omitted.

Later in his journal, he mentioned writing a book entitled The Fall of the Giants. I wanted to read it next, so I could perhaps deduce why his journal was incomplete. I began searching the library.

Serena entered and stood next to me, rubbing my head to mess up my hair which hung loosely over my shoulders. "Hi," she greeted with a smile.

"Hi," I repeated.

She glanced over the large shelf of books before us. "What are you looking for?" she asked.

"I read the journal of Ariana's grandfather. He was once head of the council. In his journal, he mentioned writing a book called The Fall of the Giants. I can't seem to find it."

"Perhaps someone is reading it," she answered.

"Perhaps. I was thinking it may hold the answer for why there are missing months in his journal."

"Hmm," she thought for a moment. "Do you believe someone is trying to hide information that he recorded?"

"Yes, I believe so."

A look of deep concern fell over her face. "Since the destruction of Magestice, battles among the races have escalated to all-out war. They feel that the council has lost its ability to maintain order. They are defending their borders and fighting to expand."

I leaned against the arm of a chair, shaking my head. "What is the council doing to stop Magnus and return peace to the world?"

Serena walked over and took a seat across from me, so I sat down too. "Half of the council has gone to negotiate with the four races that are at war." Her tone suggested that she believed the negotiations would fail. "The satyrs have attacked the centaurs, and the dwarves have gone to war with the goblins."

"Out of curiosity," I leaned forward in my chair, "which of the council members volunteered to put an end to the fighting?"

"Ariana left to speak with the centaurs and satyrs. Kildren is speaking with the goblins, and Drakuss the dwarves."

"Hmm," I thought, rubbing my bottom lip, remembering that they were the council members that seemed to disapprove of Ian's ruling. My eyes met Serena's. "Do you believe they will put an end to the bloodshed?" I asked her bluntly.

She exhaled heavily before answering. "The dwarves and goblins have fought over the mountains for centuries, and the satyrs and centaurs have fought for forests even longer. The dragons have intervened many times before, but these races absolutely hate one another. Whether they fight merely to expand their borders, or there is another reason just beneath the surface, I hold no hope negotiations will succeed." Her frustration was clearly seen across her brow as she pounded a fist on the chair arm. "They will not stop until their enemy is obliterated."

Suddenly the palace shook with a boom! Serena and I ran to the library window and saw

Magnus, in dragon form, flying into the palace wall. His army covered the ground, and dragons filled the sky.

We ran out of the library and looked down to the first floor of the palace. We saw Ian directing people out the main entrance.

Mya the Green and Gwyneth the Blue flew up the center of the building. They were in their elf forms but used their dragon wings to fly. Once they broke through the magical skylight, they changed fully into their dragon forms to engage Magnus in aerial combat.

Magnus had already stopped flying into the building. He was waiting on who will come out to challenge him. He saw the two council members coming out to face him, so he flew toward them. Gwyneth opened her mouth. Her teeth sparked with electricity, and a bolt of lightning arced toward Magnus. He banked left and rolled over the bolt. When he felt that he was close enough, he breathed in deeply and blew fire at them. Gwyneth had barely enough time to protect herself with a Resist Fire spell. Mya wasn't so lucky. Her charred body fell to the earth.

"Gwyneth," Magnus called out to her, "join me, and I will make you queen of an entire continent," he told her proudly.

Gwyneth held her position, flapping her wings to stay aloft, well above the fighting below. "And turn away from my duties, maintaining peace in the world? NEVER!"

Magnus shook his head. "Like Ian, you fail to see past the present."

"And I will fight by Ian's side until the end," she declared as she retreated to find him.

Magnus spoke aloud but not enough for her to hear. "The end, my dear, is already upon you."

Serena and I ran down the spiraling hallway but stopped when we saw vampires and werewolves searching the rooms as they made their way up. Serena grabbed my hand and pulled me to the railing, "Quickly, this way." We both looked up to see dragons outside circling the roof, waiting for someone to come out.

"Um, I don't think we want to go that way either," I told her with a laugh.

Serena then looked at one of the vertical windows that ran the height of the palace. She turned back to me with a sly grin. "Do you love me?" she asked.

"Yes," I answered, excited by what I saw she was about to do.

She kissed me on the nose, and we ran toward the huge window. She threw out an open palm, cracking the window with telekinetic force. She charged through it, taking me with her! As we fell, she pulled me close. Her dragon wings sprouted from her back, and she flew us away from the palace.

We flew over the palace gardens which were teeming with Magnus' army of skeleton warriors and bone golems. They were fighting all who tried to escape.

Ian fought his way out of the main entrance, into the heavy rain, and looked up to see Gwyneth approaching. Ian caught a scent in the air. He quickly spun around to see two werewolves leaping to attack him. He breathed frost at them. Both werewolves froze and shattered across the ground at his feet.

Ian charged through a large group of skeletons, breaking their rusty swords and shattering their bodies. He began changing into his dragon form as he continued to run; his growing body trampled more and more skeletons. When he finished his transformation, he spotted a large group of zombies making their way to the palace. Ian froze dozens of Magnus' undead, and whipped his tail to break them into pieces.

While still flying, Gwyneth sent a bolt of lightning to the ground and directed it through several zombies. Their bodies exploded on contact.

Ian spread his wings and joined Gwyneth in the air.

Magnus had been hovering away from the palace to draw them out.

When they felt they were close enough, Ian and Gwyneth held their position. Ian's voice rang out to Magnus. "You may have destroyed the World Council Palace, but you have not destroyed its council."

Ariana, Drakuss, and Kildren returned from their negotiations and were flying up behind Ian and Gwyneth. They were in elf form but flew using their dragon wings. Ian noticed them coming. He turned his attention back to Magnus. "It's over, Magnus. Surrender," he ordered.

"You are correct, Ian, in that I have not destroyed the council," Magnus said, "but it is not my intention to destroy it."

The three approaching council members

transformed fully into their dragon forms.

"It is my intention to become its leader," Magnus added with a devilish grin.

Ian gasped as he realized that he had been caught in a trap. "DIVIDE!" he yelled out to Gwyneth. Ian folded his wings and dropped but Gwyneth didn't react quickly enough. Drakuss and Kildren flew straight into her with their claws.

Ian leveled out just above the tree tops. He circled to help Gwyneth only to see her lifeless body fall.

Ian flew high into the sky. The three defected council members followed him.

Magnus headed toward the palace to help his small army of dragons kill the opposing younger dragons while the rest of the council took care of its former leader.

Ian flew up into the thick clouds, out of sight. It was sunny above the rain.

Ariana fell back to let the other two dragons go in first.

Just above the cover of clouds, Ian waited for them. As the first one broke through, Ian started breathing frost. Kildren and Drakuss flew into the trap and were iced over. They began their long fall back to the earth.

Ian flew over the clouds before dropping through. He saw Ariana waiting for him in the distance. "Why, Ariana?" he asked. "Why have you turned against me? I am your friend."

"This has nothing to do with friendship," she answered. "Our duty is to keep the peace and save lives, is it not?" she posed her own question.

Ian was hurt by her words. "It is but not like this," he said with tears in his eyes.

"To keep the peace and save lives, we must eliminate the problem before it becomes one," she stated coldly.

"But Ariana—"

"I have made my decision!" she cut him off before flying at full speed to engage him in combat.

Ian closed his eyes for a moment. He took a deep breath and exhaled. His entire body glowed with a blue aura. Just at that moment, Ariana breathed fire at him. The fire didn't harm him because of his protective aura, but he couldn't see either. She flew into him clawing and biting. She wrapped her tail around him to keep him from using his wings. They fell through the pouring rain. Ariana sank her teeth into Ian's neck.

He yelled out in pain. He used both his hands to break one of her wings, and she released her bite. He breathed in as deeply as he could, pulled loose from her tail, and blew a massive cone of frost into her face. She was engulfed. Ian flapped his wings to hold his altitude and watched Ariana spiral downward.

He made his way back and breathed frost across the undead army that surrounded the palace. Hundreds were frozen in an instant. As Ian came around for another pass, he saw Magnus and other dragons attacking all who opposed them. He flew toward Magnus to end the war.

Magnus spotted him. Two Blue Dragons saw Ian coming, and they flew up next to Magnus. "I will hold his attention," he told them. "You two, make your way around the palace and attack him from behind."

"Yes, Magnus," the two dragons said in unison as they followed their orders.

Magnus flew toward Ian.

"This ends now, Magnus!" Ian yelled.

"We'll see," Magnus said with a grin.

Ian breathed in deep and blew frost at him. Magnus breathed fire to shield himself from the frost, but he didn't take as big a gulp of air as Ian. He wouldn't be able to hold off the attack for very long, so he took human form, keeping his dragon wings, to not be such a large target. He pulled his wings in tight and dropped below the frost.

The frost attack stopped, and both Ian and Magnus sped toward each other. Magnus summoned an ethereal lance at the last second, but Ian reacted quick enough to pull back and claw at him. Magnus turned his lance to deflect the attacks as best as he could. Ian then whipped his tail, striking Magnus and knocking him into the palace wall. Ian breathed in deeply again to catch Magnus off guard. Just before releasing his chilling breath attack, the two Blue Dragons that Magnus sent around the palace appeared and blasted Ian with lightning. Ian convulsed as he was held with electricity. Magnus sprang into flight from the palace wall; his lance set on Ian. The two Blue Dragons ceased their attack, and Magnus pierced Ian's chest with the lance. Ian gasped, and Magnus let him fall.

Magnus returned to his massive Red Dragon form and let out a thunderous roar, signaling victory to his army.

A young White Dragon in Magnus' army noticed us flying away from the battle.

"It may be best to make our escape through the forest," Serena said to me, fearing an aerial battle while carrying me. She landed at the forest's edge and took hold of my hand. "Come on," she said desperately as she pulled me into the forest.

The dragon flew just above the treetops, breathing frost. The trees blackened and wilted as they shielded us from his attacks. The dragon took the form of an elf and dropped down into the forest to chase us on foot.

"Why are we running?" I asked through a chuckle. "There are two of us and only one of him. I think we can take him."

We stopped running and turned to fight the young dragon. Two vampires ran up to assist him.

"Um, now I'm thinking we should've kept running," I told her as I summoned an ethereal blade from each fist.

The two vampires each summoned an ethereal sword and attacked me.

Serena spat a quick fireball at the dragon. He dodged by rolling beneath it, and Serena leaped at him.

The vampire on my left took a swing at my neck. I blocked the attack and forced his sword to the ground. I defended against two attacks from the other vampire. I then kicked the one on my left in the face, knocking him back.

Both Serena and the White Dragon faced each other as elves but peered through dragon eyes. They forced each other's face away to protect themselves from a breath attack. Serena kneed him in the groin, elbowed him across the nose, and shoved him down. She breathed fire at him, but he rolled back on his hands and pushed himself up into the trees. He breathed frost at her from the branches, but it only made steam from meeting her fire. The steam made it impossible to see. He sprang from branch to branch to get a better view of his prey.

I brought a blade up to protect myself from the vampire on my left. I blocked an attack from my right and then punched my left side attacker in the face with a blade. I finished him off by decapitation, but this small victory cost me. I screamed out as the remaining vampire took my left arm just above the elbow. My enemies seemed to have greater control over using a sword in their hand as opposed to a blade extending from the fist.

The young dragon dropped from the trees behind Serena. She turned in time to see him breathe frost. She released an unnerving scream as she froze over. He took a closer look at her for a moment, taking in his victory, before pushing her over. She fell and shattered across the ground.

I knew my dear Serena had fallen, but I did not stop; I could not. I attacked the vampire but all my attempts were blocked. The vampire flipped over me. I changed my ethereal blade into a sword to gain more range of motion with my wrist and blocked his attack. I forced his sword down, spun, and took his head off.

I now faced the young White Dragon, still in elf form. I felt weak from the blood loss of my severed arm, but it seemed to be closing off and healing fairly quickly. I released my sword, so it dissipated.

He circled me slowly, hissing and whipping a

forked tongue. He breathed frost at me, but I forced my open hand out, directing the surrounding rain to him. I turned his frost against him, and he froze to a stop. I began to circle him, now that I had him trapped. I saw the shattered remains of my friend scattered across the ground, and my hatred built.

"Why couldn't you just let us go?" I asked him, expecting no answer. "We tried to leave peacefully. Why couldn't you just let us go?" I yelled in his face.

His eyes suddenly moved to look at me.

Magnus, in his human form, ran up just in time to see me punch the frozen dragon's head, breaking it from his body.

"I am truly sorry that I couldn't make it here in time to help you," Magnus apologized to me.

I looked at him in anger, and through gritted teeth, I asked, "To help me?" The pouring rain washed my crimson tears down my neck. My whole body shook with anger and adrenaline. The rain droplets and the world around me seemed to slow down. I could no longer hold my calm, and I snapped, bolting toward Magnus like lightning! Catching him off guard with my burst of speed and strength, I hit him with a hard, right hook. It knocked him back several yards, and I was on him in a flash.

Magnus telekinetically threw me back to buy enough time to generate a force field to protect himself from my rage. He gritted his teeth as his nose began to bleed, trying to maintain his shield.

I finally stopped pounding at the force field and stepped away from him. Taking a deep breath, time returned to normal.

"I am sorry," Magnus apologized again,

releasing his force field and getting up from the wet ground. "You must believe me."

"Why?" I asked bitterly. "Why are you sorry? Why would you want to help me? Why did you not burn me years ago when you had the chance, and rid me of this torturing existence? I am alone to face the ages. My friends, my family, my loved ones, they are all gone." I bent down to touch Serena's frozen face with a shaking hand. I pulled away with a clenched fist, and in a flash, I was gone.

I ran as fast as I could through forests, through villages, and across oceans to catch the sun, but I was not fast enough. The sun stayed just out of my reach, over the horizon.

What was I doing? I was the only one who could release Kel's spirit. I gave up chasing the sun and fell to my knees in the middle of a small human city. I screamed out as loud as I could. No one heard my scream, but they felt it. Everyone in the city threw their hands up to their ears. They seemed to be frozen in time for a moment before they fell. Blood ran from their eyes, ears, nose, and mouth. No one survived. I fell face forward in the dirt, exhausted from all that had happened.

CHAPTER XI

AN UNEXPECTED VISITOR

My home was magically lit by crystal orbs that I had collected after the destruction of the World Council Palace. A millennium had passed since the war, and I had walked the Earth alone, creeping through the shadows, watching the human race prosper. They had destroyed great forests to make way for cities as they continued to multiply. I passed through their world unseen, feeding, and taking what I needed, but I always returned underground.

Serena's old home had become my home, and it would remain mine as long as I felt safe here in the mountains of the country called Romania. I had long since cleaned it up, clearing out tree roots and replacing broken blocks, so it no longer leaked when it rained. I had filled its rooms with things such as a bureau for clothing, shelves for books, and a couple of writing desks. My arm had grown back within a week of being severed, so I was not hindered in anyway.

I sometimes sat at my desk for days, writing in my journal of things I saw or did during my travels. I had seen humans from a different perspective. They may be a filthy barbaric race, but they created complex social structures and showed a great desire for self-expression like the elves once did. I saw now the potential Magnus saw in them.

Since frequenting human cities, I had picked up playing the guitar. I loved to transfer my emotions into music. I had found it to be very therapeutic, especially after the life I had endured. Of course, no one had heard me play; I did not want to draw attention to myself. I would, however, stop to listen to others. Sometimes, when a person was trying to play a song, and it didn't quite sound right, I would ever so slightly adjust their tuning. They never saw me, but they were happy that the song finally sounded good.

I had also been drawing out scenes from memory. I didn't have enough wall space to neatly hang all my drawings, so I rotated them whenever I was in the mood. Right now, I had up a picture of my mother collecting water from the stream in a large bowl, the sun rising over the mountains of Sungrove, a view of the World Council Palace from the gardens, and a picture of Tess curled up, sleeping on my pillow.

I was working on a statue, as I so often did. My home was filled with familiar faces from my past. Some of the statues were of people that I loved with all my heart. Others, well, I would like to have kept their spirit from entering the splendor of the Sun. Sometimes I would fill the pool with hot water and just sit for hours, staring at a statue, imagining what happened in this person's life to make them who they were.

I sat on a wooden stool, molding the slender arms of what would be a marble statue of Tess. I was making her my height, just as I always wished she could be. "Just as I wished," my thoughts forced themselves aloud, breaking through my lips as a whisper. "I wish that, once I finish molding you, you would awaken."

I heard the sound of stone moving! For a moment, I thought my wish had been granted, and the statue before me had been given life, but alas, I was wrong. The sound was coming from outside. It was the stone covering the entrance that was being moved. Who knew that I was here? Could it be that Sylvia had returned? My excitement grew as I heard the rusty doors open. I listened for the first footsteps to fall upon the stone steps and smelled the air for the scent of who approached. A deep sigh escaped me as I returned to my work, for I knew who had come.

Magnus walked slowly down the hall as he looked over all the statues, admiring the detail of each. The statues were lined up evenly along both sides of the hall. The first two were of Lily and Kip, my mother and father. The next two were of me and Kelena. Then there was an empty space on one side and Trevor, who was once Kel's boyfriend, on the other. I planned to put Tess in the empty space. The last two statues lining the hall were of Sylvia and Serena.

Upon entering the main room, Magnus saw that there were many more statues. I didn't acknowledge his presence. I continued molding as he looked over my previous works. In the center of the room, on a marble pedestal in the pool, I had placed the first statue that I made of me, Kelena, and Tess.

Magnus made his way around as if in a museum, looking over fine works of art. There were statues for each member of the World Council. Magnus finally spoke as he continued to look over my work. "You know, for centuries, I believed things like this should be destroyed. I thought that humans shouldn't find proof that they are not the dominate species on the planet. I had ordered everything that wasn't crafted by human hands to vanish without a trace."

He saw that I had also sculpted statues of Yuri, Artimes, Dirk, Byron, Veronica, and one of a werewolf. The werewolf stood the tallest of all at about 7'.

"Villages were burned, homes destroyed," Magnus continued, "entire civilizations wiped out."

I stopped sculpting, remembering running back to Sungrove to find it a smoldering ruin.

Magnus found a statue of him in the group. I had sculpted him holding a miniature of the World Council Palace in the palm of his hand. He was holding it up to the sky and looking at it as if it was a priceless treasure that he had acquired. Magnus studied it a bit longer than the others before stepping over to view my current project. He looked back to my first statue, recognizing the fairies were the same. He never met Tess but saw that she was very dear to me. "But now," he added to his previous statement, "after seeing you hiding from the world, creating such beauty, I think they should be saved. I think these works of art should be kept as a reminder of our past, and our lost loved ones will never truly die."

I breathed deeply to hold back the tears. "Why are you here?" I asked as I finally turned on my stool to look at him.

"I've come to give you purpose," he stated with a big smile, "to offer you a seat among my council."

I failed to see his logic behind this. "But I don't support your cause," I told him. I was confused why he would ask me to join his council after his armies took away everything that was dear to me.

"And that is why I'm asking this of you," he explained. "I need a fresh voice among the council. I need someone who views the world differently." He walked over to look at my statue of Ian.

"I don't care anymore, Magnus," I told him, my voice hollow and cold. "How did you find me here anyway?"

"I've known you lived here for ages," he boasted, walking across the water in my pool toward the center statue. "My horses told me when they returned to Magestice," he admitted, reaching out to touch Kelena's face.

"Don't touch her!" I barked, standing from my stool.

He obeyed, pulling his hand away just shy of touching her cheek. "What are you going to do once you've sculpted everyone you've ever met and grow bored with drawing?" he asked as he crossed the pool. "What are you going to do once these halls are full?"

I looked around the room at all the statues and saw that my home was nearly full already.

"Will you please give it some thought?" he asked sincerely. "I would very much like to see you on the council."

I turned my gaze away from my creations to the floor. "I . . . I will give it some thought," I finally answered, looking back at Magnus.

"Thank you," he said with a smile and a bow. "Our next scheduled meeting will be at dawn, ten days from now, in Delhi. I do hope to see you there." He began to leave but stopped in the hallway, turning to look back at me. "Kieran," he said, drawing my attention, "don't let the past destroy you."

I looked at Kel's statue. I heard Magnus close the doors behind him and cover them with the large stone. "Strange that he would take an interest in me now," I said to the statue. I sat to relax and think. "If he wanted to kill me, he would have done it long ago." I stared at her statue, remembering Magnus killing Artimes instead of me. "Was he saving me to become a pawn in his game? Is there something I can offer that Artimes could not?"

I rubbed my chin, running a finger across my lip. I then remembered how Magnus turned half of the council against Ian because Ian didn't share his vision. "He molded them as I have molded these statues, but where I used my hands, he used carefully selected words. Magnus couldn't possibly win a war against the dragons of the World Council. If he had a vision of the human race becoming the dominate species on the planet, he must also see the steps needed to reach that future. He would have seen that he needed the council on his side instead of standing against him. I imagine he realized this a bit too late since he was defeated and imprisoned for his first attempt to exact his plan." I paused a moment as an answer struck me. "To exact his plan," I repeated. "Perhaps his vision of the future was not a vision at all. Perhaps it was designed."

I sat quietly for a while, thinking about how the world had changed over the last thousand years. Humans still fought one another and died of diseases, but they are much safer than they were. They are not hunted for food by goblins and ogres. They are not being robbed or abducted by satyrs. They are not shot on sight by the centaurs. Nor are they being killed by the dwarves for venturing too deep into the mountains.

I wondered what Magnus planned to do. Would he wage war against the other races? Did he wish to hunt down those who once lived in the Earth but now walked amongst man, using magic to conceal themselves? Could I save them by taking a seat on Magnus' council, or would I find myself following his orders to hunt them down?

"I need to move," I whispered. "He knows where I live, and I don't like that. Even if I join his council, I need my things where I feel they are safe. I would hate to return and find my home destroyed as it was long ago."

I stood from my chair, rolled my pants legs up, and took a seat at the edge of the pool, letting my feet hang in the water. I leaned back on my hands how the statue of Kelena and I were positioned.

"Maybe I will move to where the humans are calling the New World," I said with a bit of optimism. I looked around the room at all my things. "But how will I move all this?" I asked myself aloud, knowing that I couldn't carry each piece individually across the ocean. "I could really use Sonido's teleportation spell right about now," I said with a chuckle. "I might be able to load my things on one of the human's sailing vessels bound for America, but I still can't do that in less than ten days." I sat up, resting my arms in my lap, thinking of another course of action. "Well, like I said earlier, if he wanted to kill me, he would have done it long ago. The same goes for destroying my home. I will go to India and find out why he needs me on his council. I will worry about moving when I return." I pulled my feet out of the water and stood. "Perhaps I will learn a spell that can help me while I'm there." I returned to my wooden stool and continued shaping Tess' arms.

It was early morning when I entered the Indian city of Delhi. A magnificent temple lay in the distance. Cloaked in white, I made my way through the city toward the temple, passing through the crowded streets with ease. I walked up to the temple's large double doors, and they opened to me. I entered to find it brimming with color and activity. A band played music as three beautiful girls danced around the room. I noticed that everyone here looked human, but my nose told me otherwise. To not draw attention to myself, I stayed in the back of the room and kept my hood up to hide my elvish features.

"*Kieran*," I heard a familiar voice telepathically call me. I glanced around the room and spotted Magnus sitting among the crowd, looking at me.

"*I'm glad you've come*," he said to me before turning his attention to a dancer shaking her belly jewelry in his face.

When the show was over, everyone clapped

and bowed their head to the performers to show their appreciation. Magnus stood and bowed again to the performers. He kissed the hand of each of the dancers before sending them away.

Nine people stood and made their way to another room. Magnus motioned for me to follow them. He turned and walked into the room. Once inside, Magnus hugged me. "It's good to see you again, Kieran," he said to me with a big smile.

"I almost decided not to come," I admitted, "but I am curious what it is that I have to offer."

"*I will tell you after the meeting*," he telepathically promised.

The nine people that came in ahead of me had already seated themselves at a long table. Magnus took his seat at the head of the table. The two seats left were next to Magnus. I took the one on the far side.

"As we wait for one more," Magnus began, "have there been any sightings?"

A muscular, bald man lifted a finger.

"Yes, Dominic," Magnus acknowledged.

Dominic leaned forward. "There is still goblin activity within the European countries, milord. They have been spotted as stowaways on ships sailing from Ireland to France."

Magnus was clearly annoyed by this news. He gritted his teeth and forced a smile. "Yes, the goblins have proven to be a very resilient race." He took a deep breath to collect his thoughts. "Station men at the seaports of both countries immediately, and have them follow the goblins to find their nests."

Dominic bowed his head. "It will be done, milord."

Dirk walked into the room. As soon as my eyes fell on him, I sped toward him with an ethereal sword. Dirk blocked the attack with a sword of his own.

"Where is my sister's heart?" I yelled.

"I'm keeping her from going to the Sun," he told me with a smile, "or whatever nonsense you Woodland Elves believe." He bit his tongue and spat in my face. "I'm afraid you won't be going either."

Magnus stood. "Kieran! Dirk! Stop this now, and take your seats!" he ordered.

With hatred burning in my eyes, I did as Magnus ordered. I pulled my sword away from Dirk and took a few cautious steps back. Dirk kissed at me and laughed, trying to provoke me into attacking him again here in the council chamber and against Magnus' orders.

Magnus gave Dirk a hug before returning to his seat.

Dirk flashed me a smile, but I looked away, taking a deep breath to calm myself. I hated him! With every fiber of my being, I hated him. If I had the power to snap him out of existence right now, he would be gone.

"Now that everyone is seated," Magnus said, making a noticeable glance at me and Dirk, "let us begin. I have summoned you all here to inform you of an attack planned against us and the action that must be taken to protect ourselves and everything that we have worked for. A few years before my release, a very powerful warlock and his followers constructed a temple to study, teach, and experiment in a safe, secluded location. Those experiments are still taking place. I have gathered information that the attendants of this school are preparing for an attack against us. We need to act now to gain the upper hand."

"Who is at the head of the school now?" I asked, doing my best to keep from looking at Dirk.

"I don't know," Magnus answered. "They go to great lengths to keep any knowledge of their practices a secret. I have learned of their plan from a student I caught in Venice. I believed that the school had been destroyed, but I now know that they have continued their practices and teachings below ground, below where the temple once stood."

"Are we to follow through with normal procedures?" Dominic asked.

I looked at Dominic and then to Magnus, curious as to what were the normal procedures.

Magnus thought for a short moment before answering. "The people of France are unaware of the practicing of magic far beneath their beloved Cathedral of Reims, and I want to keep it that way. Yes, we will erase all signs of the school ever existing, but we will leave the above cathedral untouched."

"How many magic-users can we expect to find down there?" another council member asked. His long, golden locks and eyes told me that he was a Yellow Dragon.

"I don't know that either," Magnus answered with a shake of his head, "but I believe that we are the most powerful beings on this planet, and we will not fail." Magnus looked proudly at everyone at the table. "Now gather your warriors. We will attack just before dawn, two days from now."

Everyone began to leave the room, but Magnus remained seated. Dirk gave me another smile as we walked toward the door. I felt my temper rising again.

"Kieran," Magnus called to me. "I'd like to speak with you, if I may."

I turned my back on Dirk and took my seat next to Magnus.

Magnus waited for everyone to leave the room. The last council member closed the double doors behind him. Magnus was clearly happy to see that I came to the meeting. "I wanted to spend more time with you at your home but felt I shouldn't overstay my welcome."

But you were not welcome, I thought to myself. You just walked in.

"I must admit," Magnus continued, "I did check on you from time to time. I didn't enter your home, though," he assured me. "I would see signs that the stone covering the entrance had been moved. I also caught visions of you from animals that had seen you in the surrounding forest. You seemed to want to be alone, so I didn't bother you."

"It's not that I want to be alone," I began. "It's that I don't want to grow attached to someone only to see them die." I looked down at the wood grain in the table and remembered eating meals with my family.

Magnus no doubt noticed that I was in the past. "Talk to me, Kieran. Tell me what's on your mind."

"Things are different," I told him, still staring at the table but welcoming the chance to actually speak to someone. "I was just remembering sharing meals with my family in Sungrove. Now I have no family, and I can't even eat a piece of fruit without throwing it up." I lifted a hand to study it as I opened and closed my fingers. "Where, once my diet consisted of fruits, vegetables, and the occasional fish, now this body can only accept the blood of the living. From the day I was given eternal life, my body has craved fresh blood to keep it supple. My physical appearance may stay the same, but my heart is broken over the loss of all whom I loved." I finally looked at him, but there were no tears streaming down my face. I still very much missed my family and friends, but the sands of time had dried my eyes.

Magnus, though, looked on the brink of tears as he seemed to understand my loss. "That, my friend, is the price of immortality."

I thought for a moment, letting his words sink in before speaking. "You have lived well over a thousand years. Do you long for the day that you rejoin your loved ones in the Sun?"

"If there is an afterlife," Magnus began to answer, "then how do we know what awaits until we die ourselves?"

I expected to hear of his own beliefs, not to receive a question in return. "Are you saying you don't believe your family now resides in the Sun?"

"I'm just saying you should take a step back from religion, and look at it from an outside perspective."

I didn't know what to say to that. I sat back in my chair, remembering my grandfather talk about burning my grandmother's body to send her spirit to the Sun.

Magnus saw that he had stumped our conversation, so he moved on. "Well, let's get down to business, shall we?"

My vision of the past ended, and I gave

Magnus my full attention.

"Six months ago," he began, "when the last council meeting took place, one of the vampire chair holders did not attend. I believe him to be destroyed, possibly by someone that is a member of the council. I asked about the missing chair holder, but if a council member did destroy him, they maintained their composure. They did not think of destroying him, so I could not catch a glimpse of his death by reading their thoughts."

"How can I help?" I asked.

"Now that you are among the oldest, would you be interested in a seat among the World Council?" he asked me. "Of course, I will assign you an area to keep watch over, and you will have access to the council archives. All you have to do is form a council of your own, report any sightings of nonhuman races, keep all signs of those races from the humans, and attend the council meetings whenever I schedule them."

This sounded like serious business, I thought to myself. In one hand, it would be nice to have a job to do. In the other, what if I became next on the hit list?

"You don't have to answer right away," Magnus told me, since I was weighing my options. "There is something I would like to ask of you, though."

"What would that be?"

"Within that school is a very important book, and right now, I feel that I cannot trust any of the current members of the World Council. I will need you to help me find that book."

"Can you describe it to me?"

"It's a journal—Byron's journal," Magnus explained. "Not only is it a record of his life, but it also contains all the spells that he ever learned and conceived. I learned of this too from the mind of my Venetian victim."

"Byron wrote new spells?" I asked, astounded.

"He was a very powerful warlock," Magnus answered.

I thought for a moment before asking, "Where is the Venetian now? I would like to question him."

"I had to kill him," Magnus admitted. "I could not risk the knowledge that I had learned of their plan to attack. What would you like to ask him?" Magnus asked curiously.

"What was this Venetian doing out by himself to be caught by you, no less, with such important information?" I asked boldly.

Magnus' proud expression turned to one of concern.

"Smells like bait," I added suspiciously.

"But we can't wait around for them to attack," Magnus explained.

"You're right," I agreed. "We can't."

"We will just have to be extra cautious."

I didn't like this plan, but as Magnus said, we couldn't just wait around. I could have backed out. I could have gotten a wagon from a human city and begun hauling my things to a seaport, but what if Magnus failed? These warlocks could have free reign over the entire world, and I couldn't begin to imagine their plans for it. At least under Magnus' rule, the world was much more peaceful than it once was.

Hearing no objections, Magnus stood. "We have plenty of rooms here in the palace. You are welcome to stay." He placed a hand on my shoulder.

"Thank you. I will stay," I gladly accepted the invitation as we walked to the chamber doors. "And thank you for listening to me. It's been quite some time since I've had someone to talk to."

"You are very welcome," he told me with a genuine smile. "We will talk again soon. Just so you know," his tone changed, "there is to be no fighting here. Dirk knows this and will follow this rule. I expect you to do the same."

"Dirk wishes to kill me, and I don't want to die by his hand," I told him, fearing my days were numbered. "Can you help me?"

Magnus took a deep breath. "Everyone has their demons, Kieran, and everyone must face their demons alone." He opened the door and placed a hand on my back to allow me to walk in front.

We left the council chamber to once again enjoy the festivities in the main hall.

CHAPTER XII

BENEATH THE CATHEDRAL

Just before dawn, I stood with the eleven council members and their twenty-five chosen soldiers outside the Cathedral of Reims.

"It's ironic that beneath this religious temple lie practitioners of what the religion states as acts of evil," one of the vampire council members said.

"Some things are just not quite what they appear to be," Magnus said with a smile.

We followed Magnus into the cathedral and walked quietly to a back room. The monks that inhabited the church must all still be asleep. Magnus waved a hand, and a portal opened in the floor to reveal a wide, spiraling staircase. Torches on the wall of the stairwell burst into green flames to light our way. Once everyone had joined Magnus in the stairwell, he lifted a hand and closed his fingers into a fist to close the portal behind us. We walked silently down the long staircase. Every twenty steps, there was a skeleton set into the wall on both sides of the stairs. I kept a watchful eye on them as we passed, fearing they would attack us at any moment.

For nearly an hour, we walked before reaching a dark room at the bottom. It magically illuminated, revealing the room to be massive, and its high ceiling was supported by many stone columns. Once everyone cautiously entered the room, a wall magically formed to block our escape.

"I don't think this was a good idea," I whispered.

A loud boom took everyone's attention, then another and another. It was the sound of footsteps! Our faces, including Magnus', reflected shock and fear when an 80' stone golem stepped into view. It squatted down to get a closer look at us. In a slow, rumbling voice, the golem spoke. "You do not belong here." The golem then raised its right hand to swat us.

"RUN!" one of the council members yelled.

The golem swung and hit two elf vampires across the room against the wall. The others had moved out of the way in time. The golem pounded a Green Dragon, still in human form, with its fist.

The dragons tried their breath attacks on the golem, but it only seemed to cloud its vision. It pounded at others, but its accuracy was off. The golem tried to step on them.

Two female dragons changed into their true forms: one was a Black Dragon and, the other, a Blue. The other dragons, including Magnus, revealed just their wings. The golem swatted and missed all the dragons except one. It caught the female Black Dragon by the neck with its left hand. The golem then grabbed her body with its right hand and pulled her apart at the base of the neck. It threw the two pieces to each side.

The werewolves climbed up it as a diversionary tactic so the vampires could try to cut through it at the ankles with ethereal swords, but it was too big. It was hard to get close enough to do any damage without it trying to stomp us.

Magnus cast a Transmute Stone to Mud spell at it, but only a very small portion liquefied. The spell didn't affect it enough to even slow it down. "Damn!" he yelled out in failure. "It must be stacked with resistances."

Some of the dragons flew into the back of it to try to make it fall forward. It lost its balance and went down on one knee. It put its left hand down to steady itself and began to stand back up.

Dominic transformed into a werewolf and leaped at the golem's face. He slashed at one of its eyes in an attempt to blind it. Chunks of rock were chipped away.

The golem knocked Dominic to the floor and punched straight down on him. When it raised its fist, Dominic looked like a bloody paste.

Dirk cast the same Transmute Stone to Mud spell that Magnus had earlier, but Dirk targeted the floor at the golem's feet. The large stone blocks that made up the floor turned soft, and the golem began to sink. It didn't sink all the way down but far enough to not pose a threat. The golem grunted and growled as it tried to break free but couldn't.

"Great job, Dirk!" Magnus congratulated.

"Great job."

"We didn't seem to be winning by trying to attack it directly," Dirk explained, "so I thought I would try an indirect attack."

We paid our respects to the dead and magically incinerated them before following Magnus to two large doors at the far end of the room. With a wave of his hand, he telekinetically opened them. Behind the doors lay another set of spiraling stairs. Green flames once again lit our way.

This stairwell didn't seem half as long as the first. At the bottom, we found a long hallway. It was dark, except for a soft green light at the very end. There were also four corridors, two on either side, also lit by the magical light.

Magnus turned to look at his army and sent us a telepathic message to keep as quiet as possible. "*Divide into five groups. Kieran, Ryan, Nadia, Demetrius, and Elizabeth, you all are with me. Remember: quickly and quietly. Now go.*"

Each of the four other groups took a corridor. I stayed close to Magnus as our team went straight down the hall. I'm glad Dirk was with another group. If he was in mine, I may have been tempted to kill him myself.

We tried sneaking, but once inside the large room at the opposite end of the hall, another wall closed off our exit. There was a stairwell on the left and the right side of the room. Three warlocks were floating in front of a table on the opposite side of the room. All three warlocks were vampires. The one in the middle was the Dark Elf Byron! He was wearing a dark red cloak. The other two were wearing a royal blue and a forest green-colored cloak.

At almost a whisper, Magnus said, "Byron lives!"

Byron was concentrating on casting a spell. He had his fingers hooked and the knuckles from both hands pressed together in front of him. His head was bowed, but he kept his eyes on us.

The green-cloaked warlock was also concentrating on a spell, but his fists were clenched and kept at his sides.

The warlock wearing the royal blue cloak pulled a glass flask from inside his cloak. The flask was filled with an icy blue liquid. He removed the cork, and the liquid rose out.

"*We shouldn't wait around for them to cast their spells*," Magnus ordered. "*Attack!*"

I summoned an ethereal sword as we ran toward the warlocks.

Byron pulled his hands apart to cast his spell. The floor cracked open right behind Magnus. Demetrius, a Red Dragon in the form of a winged human, tried to fly over the crevasse but was sucked in. Everyone else made it by running around the crevasse before it split across the entire floor. Byron moved his knuckles back together to close the floor. It closed without a trace.

The liquid from the flask exploded into five globules toward us. Magnus dodged a globule, but the blue-cloaked warlock telekinetically steered the globule back to Magnus, and it hit him. His body frosted over, and his speed was slowed tremendously.

Ryan transformed into a werewolf as he ran across the room. He leaped onto the green-cloaked warlock, tearing into him. The warlock didn't even have time to cast his spell. The globule of blue liquid hit Ryan. He turned his attention to the blue-cloaked warlock. He fought the Slow spell to get to him.

Byron saw the werewolf slowly making his way to them and began concentrating on another spell.

Elizabeth, an elf, swung an ethereal sword at the globule aimed at her. She split it in two which didn't help her. She was hit with both halves. She frosted over and fell to the floor. She didn't shatter, but she was frozen stiff.

I flashed my left hand at the oncoming globule. The blue liquid froze solid, hit my hand, and shattered harmlessly on the floor.

Nadia had transformed into some kind of werelion. She swatted at the globule, but that wasn't a good idea; she frosted over.

Byron flew toward Ryan like a nightmarish specter and touched him with both hands. Still fighting the Slow spell, Ryan cringed and began to fall to his knees in slow motion. Byron began concen-trating again.

I reached the blue-cloaked warlock, which was the closest to me. I leaped into the air and released a strong war cry as I came down on the warlock's head with my sword. The warlock was cleaved in two!

Ryan was on his knees, changing back to human form, holding his stomach. His face reflected extreme pain. He let out a slow, deep yell as his guts began to come out through his navel. The spell worked faster as the Slow spell wore off. It was wearing off everyone.

I turned to Byron, but before I could get to him,

he flashed a hand at me. I was held back by a force field. I tried to break through it, but he was too strong.

"How about showing some respect by not disturbing my concentration," Byron said with a regal smile. He made a circular motion with his index finger to create a tornado around me. The tornado spun me away from him and toward the stairs.

Just as he sent me away, he cast the spell that he had been concentrating on. A shadowy apparition took shape and flew toward Nadia and Elizabeth.

The tornado beat me into the walls as it spun me down the stairs. I spun over halfway down a hallway before the spell ended. Once the tornado could no longer hold me up, I fell to the floor. I tried to pick myself up, but my equilibrium was off.

"Oh, I feel sick," I uttered. My eyes rolled back into my head, and I vomited blood. "Ugh. Sick. I'm no good to the mission like this. I need to lie here until the room stops spinning."

Within seconds of lying my head down, two giant eyeballs flew into the room. They looked around and spotted me on the floor. They zipped over to study me. I moved to get up, and the eyes nervously flew out of the hall. I tried to stand but stumbled a bit. I used the wall to regain my balance. I tried to make my way back toward the stairs, but the hallway was quickly filled with more of the temple's inhabitants. I was surrounded by all sorts of nightmarish creatures blocking my escape, some that I had only read about from books in the council library.

The first creatures that caught my attention were trolls. There were a few types of trolls in the world. These were tall, thin, and gray, with sharp teeth and claws. They had short, pointy ears, a long chin, and a long, hooked nose.

There were also imps here. They flew from shoulder to shoulder to get a closer look at me. They looked like fairy-sized goblins with leathery wings that were almost too small to carry them.

Then there were the Dark Elves. With skin the color of ash and white, silky hair, they were the unspoken relatives of my race.

Now the ghouls were a chilling lot to look upon. Their hairless, bone-white skin appeared tightly pulled over a sinewy frame, and they moved with an odd gait. They had a short nose, pointy ears, and their eyes, their eyes traveled over my body. Perhaps they were sizing me up for a meal, but from what I remembered reading, ghouls preferred the decaying flesh of a corpse. Like vultures circling a wounded animal, maybe they sensed death approaching. A smile cracked my face as I thought how tough I should be to chew for someone as old as I.

One Dark Elf stepped from the crowd. "What is your business here, cousin?" he asked with a venomous tone.

"I am here with the World Council to meet with Byron," I answered calmly. They didn't seem to know what was going on upstairs, so there was no reason to involve them, especially since I was alone down there.

He noticed blood on my lips and an imp sniffing the small puddle of blood behind me. "That doesn't explain why you are vomiting on our floor."

Everyone began to close in on me.

"Tell us why you are really here," he ordered.

I glanced around at how many were in the hall.

There were well more than I could handle alone, and I was sure there were others. I didn't think they were going to just let me stroll out of there, but I needed to check on Magnus and the rest of the team. They weren't fairing so well when I was suddenly wisped away by the wind.

My Dark Elf interrogator grabbed me by the mouth and pulled my attention back to him. "Tell us why you are here!" he repeated with a sterner tone.

"I don't have time for this," I spat as I swung an open hand around and telekinetically cleared a path to the stairs. I sped out of the hallway and up the stairs to rejoin the fight against Byron.

When I reached the top of the stairs, I saw Magnus on his knees and Byron with his hands on Magnus' head. Byron's hands were glowing blue because he was using an advanced mind reading spell.

The rest of the team lay dead on the floor, except Dirk. He wasn't helping Magnus escape; he stood with Byron! It must have been Dirk who killed the council member, but why? Perhaps I could figure this out later, if I could get out of here alive, but right now, I had to stop this! They hadn't yet noticed me, so maybe I could take Dirk out before Byron realized I was there.

Just as I began to move through the shadows toward Dirk, I saw him turn to Byron and summon an ethereal sword. Byron snapped out of a trance as he searched through Magnus' mind. He quickly turned his attention to Dirk, but before he could cast a spell, Dirk cut off his head. Both Byron's and Magnus' bodies crumpled to the floor.

I ran to Magnus to see if he was okay. He was

alive but too weak to get up.

Dirk paid little attention to me as he squatted next to Byron's severed head. With a triumphant smile, he said "Byron, Byron, Byron. You had time to move out of reach, but then you have always relied on magic just a little too much."

As blood continued to run from Byron's head, his mouth moved as if trying to form words. "Why would you do this?" he said inaudibly.

Dirk read his lips and answered. "I want the same thing you want, and nothing will get in my way." His serious tone broke into laughter. "But you should have seen this coming, sorcerer." He stood, setting his sights on Magnus. His expression once again turned dark. "It should've been obvious that I crave power."

I stood to protect Magnus as he lay helpless on the floor.

Dirk leaped in to attack. I summoned a sword just in time to block it, and we pushed against each other's blade. He headbutted me, and I stumbled back. Before I could retaliate, he telekinetically threw me against the wall.

Dirk crouched next to Magnus and bit into him, draining him of blood and knowledge.

The creatures from the lower temple level entered the room. "Our master has been killed!" the Dark Elf said for all to hear.

"Dirk killed him! Dirk killed Byron!" I yelled out as I got up from the floor. If I couldn't stop Dirk then maybe we could outnumber him.

The elf glanced at a couple of ghouls standing next to him. He snapped his fingers and pointed at me. The two ghouls leaped across the room and grabbed hold of me.

"Dirk willingly gave Byron his blood so he could learn from it," the elf told me. "He would never—"

"Read Byron's dying mind!" I cut him off, remembering how Serena caught visions from the mind of the dead werewolf.

Like a lion guarding his meal, Dirk pulled Magnus across the floor as he continued to feed. His eyes glanced around the room to see that there were too many for him to fight off.

The elf walked toward Byron's severed head. He crouched next to it to see what happened for himself.

Knowing that he would see the truth, Dirk released Magnus. He shot me an angry look before running over to a big table covered with books, scrolls, and various ingredients for spell casting. He took the biggest book, which I sensed was Byron's journal, but he was quickly covered with imps. One fought to pull the book from his hands while others bit, clawed, and cast spells at him. A fireball to the face caused him to lose his grip on the book, and he stumbled back empty-handed. He summoned another sword and cut down three imps. The other imps cowered within the group. The magical wall that formed to keep us from escaping was no longer there, but now the way was blocked by Dark Elves and trolls.

"Release your weapon, Dirk, and surrender," the Dark Elf leader demanded.

Dirk stood at the ready, watching everyone closely. "You know that I won't do that, Sirithan," he told him.

"I know, but I thought I would at least offer you a chance to surrender peacefully."

Dirk began to laugh. "Peacefully," he repeated. "There is no peace." He then threw his sword at the nearest troll, impaling it in the chest. He summoned a sword for each hand and cut a swath through everyone blocking his escape.

With a nod of his head, Sirithan sent the rest after him. He then put one hand on Byron's forehead and held his left hand out. A ghostly projection of the battle against Byron played out for the few still present. The scenes of the fight that I missed showed Nadia and Elizabeth being clawed and bitten by the apparition Byron summoned. Their slow attacks passed right through it, having no effect. The elf Elizabeth was easily killed by the wraith, but Byron commanded it to hold the werelion. It would take more than an angry spirit to kill her. Byron pulled a silver dagger from his cloak and stabbed Nadia in the chest before the Slow spell completely wore off.

The projection showed Byron release the spell that closed off the exit, and Dirk entered the room.

Magnus still fought the Slow spell, which was wearing off but not wearing off quick enough. Dirk walked up from behind and held him, so Byron could begin his energy feed. The summoned spirit dissipated as the spell duration ended, and while Byron was distracted with Magnus, Dirk decapitated him.

Sirithan released Byron's severed head, and the projection ended. "Imprison them until we capture Dirk and decide on a punishment," he told everyone.

Two Dark Elves lifted the severely weakened Magnus and dragged him away as the ghouls, which had hold of me, followed.

I yelled out to Sirithan as I was being dragged down the steps to the lower levels of the cathedral. "We believed Byron was planning to attack us! We came to prevent that attack but found that Dirk had orchestrated this whole thing to gain more power!"

Magnus and I were taken through two levels and thrown into a large, round pit in the center of the room. It was about a 40' fall, and we both hit hard on the dirt floor.

"Thanks!" I yelled out to them, but they paid no attention. They left us alone in the sparsely lit chamber. I checked Magnus to find him unconscious but alive.

There were metal doors on both sides of the pit. I tried them both but couldn't force them open. They must've been magically sealed. The only other way to escape was the way we came in. I looked up, but there appeared to be a transparent barrier over the pit. Light shimmered across an invisible surface. I jumped to test the barrier. My hands pressed against it, and I dropped back to the pit floor. Like in the World Council Palace a millennium ago, it was a one-way barrier. Accepting that there was no escape, at least for now, I laid down next to Magnus.

Days passed without a sound from above. I was trying to conserve my strength by lying there, but I could still feel my energy slowly depleting. I still needed blood.

Magnus called for me with a faint voice. "Kieran?"

I sat up to check on him. "I'm here."

"There is something that I need to tell you," he

uttered. "My name isn't Magnus, and I am not an ancient Red Dragon as everyone believes me to be. My birth name was Manius, and I am really a vampire—a human vampire."

I thought for a moment to process the information. He needed blood! I did too, but I would share what strength I had with him. I put my wrist to his mouth. He took hold of my arm and sank his teeth in. I felt my body grow weaker at a faster rate. My heart pumped blood, but he took it. My pulse quickened! I saw his eyes flash fiery red for a moment, and he released me. I pulled my arm away and examined where he bit my wrist. The mark of a vampire! I licked away the still oozing blood as the wound began to slowly heal. I couldn't afford to lose anymore. I turned my attention back to him.

He used a finger to raise his lip, so I could see his vampire fangs. They retracted, returning to an unnoticeable length. "Thank you," he told me, looking better already.

"You're welcome, Manius," I said, glad that I could help.

He stood slowly and looked around the pit that we were in. "How long have we been here?"

Before I answered his question, he asked another. "Are we the only survivors?"

"Days, maybe weeks. I'm not sure," I answered his first question. "Dirk was the one who killed the council member. He was the one who betrayed you."

"Dirk," he repeated through gritted teeth. "I should have known, but it's hard to trust any bloodsuckers. Where is he now? Did Byron use some horrible spell to end his treacherous existence?"

He already saw from the expression on my face that he was not going to like what I was about to say. "Dirk used Byron just as he used you," I began. "You mentioned that Byron was a powerful warlock and even created new spells. Dirk wanted that power for himself but first needed his help to bring you down. I imagine Byron wouldn't let Dirk feed on him in fear that he would take all his arcane knowledge, so Dirk gave him his blood to test, knowing that he would grant himself immortality. With him being a vampire, Dirk knew that it was only a matter of time until Byron felt confident enough to stand up to you. Byron didn't trust him, but what he failed to see was that Dirk was using you as a distraction so that he could kill you both."

"That little shit," Manius responded, grinning through clenched teeth. He walked around, trying the doors, thinking over what I had just told him. "Well," he patted himself on the chest with both hands, "it's obvious that he failed, so where is he now?"

"He has escaped," I answered, hating to give him more bad news. "He killed Byron. He began feeding on you but stopped when Byron's followers tried to catch him. He tried to take the journal during his escape but left empty handed."

Manius shook his head disappointedly. "There's no telling what knowledge he gained from me, but it's good that he didn't get the journal. Byron was wise to keep his blood from Dirk."

We began to hear talking from above. I stood as the creatures that I saw earlier began gathering around the pit. I looked back at Manius. "I would like to ask you a few questions, but I don't think now is the time."

"No, but I promise you, we will have our talk," Manius assured me, "and I will tell you everything."

"That is, if we make it out of here alive," I added grimly.

He almost laughed at my despair. "I've escaped from worse predicaments," he said, reminding me that he was once imprisoned for centuries within the Earth.

The crowd divided to allow a female Dark Elf to step to the edge of the pit and look down at us. "Magnus and Kieran," she addressed us, "my name is Tamara, and I am the leader of this temple now."

"Where is Sirithan?" I asked her. "I thought he was the leader here."

With sad hesitation, she answered, "Sirithan is dead." She looked away, trying to hide her sorrow. She wiped away her tears before looking back. "Dirk is too powerful now. We cannot fight him. We have only you two to punish for the attack on our temple. Once you are dead, Magnus the Red, the world will return to the old ways. The humans will be our food and our slaves. They will no longer be protected by your rules."

"The humans are our slaves," Manius stressed. "They just don't know it because of my rules."

"We are tired of hiding, Magnus!" she exclaimed. "We cannot live by your rules! For centuries, Byron has been sending his creations out into the world without your knowing, but there is still one new race that he has not," she added, holding up a finger.

The magical seal on the large metal doors was broken, and they began to slowly creak open. It was dark within. I could only make out the heat signature of strange creatures within the rooms.

"Would you like to meet them?" Tamara asked with a sinister smile, eager to see a good pit fight.

Manius and I stood back to back in the center of the pit, facing the doors. We tried to summon ethereal swords, but nothing happened.

"Ah yes," Tamara said with a laugh. "I forgot to mention—magic doesn't work within the pit."

Manius didn't show fear, but I did, then more so when the monsters appeared. They quickly flew out of the darkness to see what was for dinner. They were 18' long, had the body of a dragon with no back legs, and the head of a bull.

"Once we set them free," Tamara said aloud, "they will multiply, and their race will be known as Minogon."

Manius and I waited until the two beasts lunged at us before we made a move. Hoping they would fly into each other, we found that they were very nimble. As I tried to jump out of the way, I was tail-whipped to the ground. Manius strafed, but the minogon grabbed him and flew straight up. It pounded him into the barrier. The spectators were startled, forgetting about the barrier keeping us in the pit. Manius was then dropped, and everyone cheered at the excitement.

With the minogon flying close behind, I ran toward the wall. I took a few steps up and sprung over the creature as it plowed into the wall. I landed on my feet, placing a hand on the ground for added balance. The minogon was knocked unconscious for the moment.

The other had landed and was clawing and butting at Manius. He grabbed one of its horns and slammed its head into the ground. The minogon shook it off and continued its attack.

I rejoined Manius, and the monster doubled its attack against us. It caught me with a horn as I tried to get behind the creature. It ripped my shirt as I was thrown to the side. I tore away the remainder of the shirt, but just as I started back to help Manius, the other beast wrapped itself around me! It had regained consciousness and was now crushing me!

Manius saw that I was in trouble, but his attacker also took him by surprise with a breath of chlorine gas! The minogon quickly slithered around outside the gas to ambush him. A few seconds passed, and Manius leaped out of the gas, over the minogon. He grabbed its tail and swung it around over his head with both hands. The spinning caused the gas to disperse. Manius slammed the minogon into a wall, killing the beast.

My eyes shut tight as I fought being crushed by the minogon. The more it constricted, the madder I became. I screamed out as I exploded from the minogon, and it fell dead to the ground. Manius was amazed at my physical strength to burst free from such a powerful creature.

To replenish our energy, we fed on them. The temple inhabitants were furious!

Manius released his meal with an idea. "Kieran, I know how we can escape. Follow me."

I stopped drinking from the dead monster and followed Manius into the darkness of one of the open rooms. We broke through the floor to face our captors. Both Manius and I summoned a sword and a shield.

The creatures tried to fight us off by throwing

fireballs and shooting bolts of magical energy. We dodged the fireballs, and the magic missiles exploded into small bursts of light when we blocked them with our shields.

We continued to make our way toward the creatures until a Dark Elf threw out a handful of powder. The powder ignited, and a firewall kept us from our enemies. Manius and I backed away from the blazing heat.

They no longer cast fireballs because they would only be absorbed by the firewall, so they sent a barrage of magic missiles through. I was lucky enough to block or dodge them, but one of the energy bolts hit Manius. It burned a hole through his right shoulder.

"Are you all right?" I asked him.

He examined the wound but didn't seem to be in any pain. "It looks worse than it really is."

"But I can see all the way through!"

"At least it's clean," he added with a smile. He looked up to see that the wall of fire didn't go all the way to the ceiling. "Are you ready to spoil their fun?"

A big grin lit my face, and we jumped over the fire.

Our enemies were surprised to see us drop in on them. Manius went one way, and I went another as we began slicing them up. Ghouls leaped at us from all directions, but we took them with ease, hacking limbs and severing heads.

We tried to cut down our enemies before they could cast spells. Some spells, such as Fireball and Magic Missile, can be cast quickly, so we had to dodge or block them. Some of the fireballs, which we dodged, hit other spellcasters, and they were burned.

A troll cast a spell on himself to double his size and pushed his way through the crowd toward me. I saw him coming, but I was forced to fight the others because I was surrounded. When the giant troll got within reach, he punched down at me. With a strafe and a spin, I severed his arm. Screaming out in pain, the troll backhanded me into the wall. I was stunned. My sword and shield dissipated.

Manius saw what had happened and leaped across the room toward the giant troll with furious anger. His shield became another sword, and he used both to stab the monster. Shrinking to its original size, the troll fell to the floor. Knowing that they can heal from almost any wound, Manius decapitated him.

Manius offered a hand to help me up. As I stood, I caught his scent; it was different. With a confused look, I said, "You're not Manius."

He thrust a dagger at my throat, but I was quick enough to catch his wrist. I pried the dagger from his hand and stabbed him in the chest with it.

"Why won't you just die already?" he spat as he became a she!

Returning to her true form, I saw that my attacker was the Dark Elf Tamara. I lowered her carefully to the floor. "I don't know how," I answered, but she was already gone.

A bright light flashed within the room, and I heard Manius yell out my name. His eyes were shut tight, and several imps were stabbing him with ornate daggers. He started spinning with his ethereal swords out. The imps were chopped up and slung away from him. Manius was badly hurt, but he continued to fight.

Another Dark Elf teleported in close and tried

to kill me with an elvish short sword. I quickly dodged the first attack and summoned a weapon. He disappeared and reappeared, each time, making a cut. Every time I swung my sword, I was too late; he had already cut me and vanished. I concentrated on using all my senses to locate where he would appear next. He appeared and I swung! My ethereal sword cut through his elvish sword and through him.

Far behind me, I heard the sound of another troll dying at the hands of Manius. I turned to see that he and I were the only two left standing. Bodies littered the room, and it had grown quiet. A sigh of relief escaped me as I released my sword.

"You all right?" Manius asked from across the room.

I looked over myself before answering. "Just a few cuts and minor burns."

Manius stepped over bodies as he made his way to me. A lightning bolt hit him from an invisible source, and he was thrown across the room!

"Manius!" I yelled out, but before I could run to him, something clamped down on my shoulder and pierced the skin! I winced as I felt something ice cold enter my veins, and then I saw it. Across the room, the light shimmered, and a creature took shape. It had a humanlike upper half and the lower half of a serpent. They were the Naga, an ancient race of subterranean snake people.

I was released, and I collapsed to the floor. The naga that attacked me had also become visible. It loomed over me, watching its venom take effect. A scream from the other took the naga's attention away from me, and it slithered to its aid.

I couldn't get up. What was wrong with me? I couldn't move! I couldn't feel my body! Manius! Manius! I was screaming, but no sound was escaping. My lips weren't moving. I couldn't even breathe. I heard Manius fighting off the nagas, but it sounded far away. Wait! I drew breath again! My body was reviving! My vampiric blood was fighting off the poison. It only took a few moments for the paralysis to be extinguished, and I was able to pick myself up. Manius needed my help.

Manius had wounded one of the creatures, and now they both had him backed against the wall. I took a deep breath to regain my focus as my blood burned off the last of the poison in my veins. My fingers grasped the handle of the ethereal sword forming in my hand, and I leaped across the room toward the naga that bit me. Just before my sword cleaved its skull, the beast turned, flashed a hand at me, and I was caught in another tornado spell. I was wisped over the large pit where Manius and I were held captive, and then the funnel cloud dissipated, dropping me in. I was not made sick this time, but the room was sure spinning. I got to my feet, holding my arms out to balance myself, and I saw the naga slip down into the pit.

With the spin of the room slowing down, I saw the naga throw its hands out at me as if casting a spell, but nothing happened. It tried again, and nothing happened. It looked at its hands in confusion.

I laughed at the beast and repeated what Tamara had said earlier. "Ah yes, I forgot to mention magic doesn't work within the pit."

Seeming to understand me, the naga grew furious. It bared its teeth and lashed its forked tongue.

It made a hissing scream as it puffed its chest, and a large menacing hood unfurled from the sides of its round, humanlike head.

My eyes grew wide as the naga's scare tactic seemed to be working.

The creature began taunting me by making quick, forward motions as it closed the distance between us.

Now how should I deal with this thing? If I fought it outside the pit, it would regain all its magical powers. If I fought it here, we were left with only our natural abilities. Well, I couldn't risk it turning invisible again. I must finish this here. I flashed my fangs and took an aggressive stance.

The naga spat venom at me! I used my quick reflexes to dodge it but realized that the venom was used as a distraction when I saw the creature lunging forward to bite me. Within mere inches of my face, I grabbed the beast's head with both hands and broke its neck.

The room was quiet again. I wondered if Manius was able to kill the other naga. I was about to call for him when I heard something moving above. I stood quietly, watching the rim of the pit for the other naga to drop in on me. I was relieved to see Manius step to the edge.

"Let's get out of here," he said to me.

Before leaving the room, we each took a robe from a couple of Dark Elves.

"I will send some people to clean this place up," Manius told me.

"So what are you going to do about the council now that its members have been killed?" I asked.

"Who will take their seats?"

"I'm not going to reform the council," he answered.

I looked at him, surprised by his answer. "There has been a World Council since the dawn of civilization. It has helped keep everything in balance so chaos doesn't run rampant. What about the goblins? What about Dirk? Will they not bring chaos? Will they not destroy what you have worked so hard to accomplish?"

"We don't need a council to take care of them," he answered coolly. "I have men hunting down goblins, and the few creatures that can't hide from the humans are too few to maintain their species. As for Dirk, well, he will show up. Besides, I believe it's time for the humans to look after themselves. Now, of course, I will take a position so that I can influence major decisions. I would hate for them to destroy themselves, but everything will be all right. Don't worry."

I exhaled my worries and nodded my head.

We entered the room where Byron was. I picked up his journal from the table and handed it to Manius.

With a bow of his head, Manius thanked me. "The world could fall into another Dark Age if this book fell into the wrong hands."

We walked back through the stone golem's chamber. The golem appeared to be frozen in time. I guessed, once its creator Byron died, it ceased to be animated.

As we entered the cathedral's back room, we heard preaching. Manius and I pulled our hoods up and put our hands in the sleeves of our robes. We walked out of a room from behind the bishop. The cathedral was full of humans listening to a story about the beginning of their existence. No one seemed to notice us because we appeared as monks. We walked up a side hall toward the exit.

The bishop was reading Genesis 4:14 through 4:17. "Behold, thou has driven me out this day from the face of the earth; and from thy face shall I be hid; and I shall be a fugitive and a vagabond in the earth; and it shall come to pass, that every one that findeth me shall slay me. And the Lord said unto him, therefore whosoever slayeth Cain, vengeance shall be taken on him sevenfold. And the Lord set a mark upon Cain, lest any finding him should kill him. And Cain went out from the presence of the Lord, and dwelt in the land of Nod, on the east of Eden. And Cain knew his wife; and she conceived, and bare E'-noch: and he builded a city, and called the name of the city, after the name of his son, E-noch . . . ."

We stopped at the door. "If Adam and Eve were the first humans, and they had two sons, Cain and Abel, where did that woman in Nod come from?" I asked him with a smile before we both burst into chuckling laughter.

"It's good to see you smile, my friend," he told me, placing a hand on my shoulder. He looked back at the mortals listening to the church service. "They have devised a story to explain their origin and what lies ahead, but they have no idea the vastness of it all," he said, more to himself than to me. He stood there for a moment, lost in his thoughts.

I whispered his name to bring him back, and

we walked out into the morning sun. With our cloaks blocking most of the sun's rays from our vampiric skin, we made for the shadows cast by buildings.

"Do you happen to know anything about teleportation?" I asked him, remembering the many statues that I needed to move.

He draped an arm over my shoulder as we walked down the city sidewalk. "I know a few tricks that may interest you," he answered with a smile.

CHAPTER XIII

A STARTLING RESEMBLANCE

Perched atop a building in New York, I watched the horse and buggies move along the streets below. The city was filled with sights, sounds, and delicious smells, the smell of warm-blooded humans on a cool April night.

I moved to what was now being called America a couple of centuries ago. Manius told me that the trick to teleporting was that I should have a clear mental image of the place where I want to go. I didn't like the idea of being out in the open waters of the Atlantic for a month, so I fed on a sailor that had just returned from the New World. His memories allowed me to teleport safely across the ocean, and it didn't take long to find a nice secluded spot in the mountains to dig a new home. It did, however, take some time to move everything from the old place to the new. I didn't realize how much I had accumulated until I had to sort through and move it all.

Right now, I was in search of an interesting meal. I don't like to drink from someone without helping them in some way, so I look for someone who has a problem that I can set right. Everyone has problems, but I mean problems like healing the sick, mending the crippled, or feeding the poor. Sometimes I even find myself on a little adventure that brings a flicker of excitement to my life.

Of course, I never let any of these people believe they were visited by a vampire. It is forbidden to draw attention to ourselves, so I am careful to always cover my tracks. I heal the bite marks and erase their memory of the encounter. I find it amusing that people are quick to say that God sent an angel to answer their prayers.

What was that sound floating on the wind? I turned my head to focus my hearing. It was the hum of a violin. The sound was beautiful. I listened for a moment, pinpointing the sound's location. I then effortlessly made my way across the city by building top, toward the beautiful music.

I located the building that the music was coming from and dropped down from the roof. I magically changed my ears to appear human, another power that I learned from Manius to better blend in. I turned the door knob, releasing the lock with a mere thought, and walked into the house. I was spellbound by what I saw. TESS! This human female resembled my long lost love. She was playing the violin with her eyes shut, swaying to the music. I quietly took a seat so that I didn't interrupt her. I noticed a wooden crucifix on the wall and a few oil paintings, but my eyes did not wander long before returning to the lovely creature standing before me.

When she finished her piece, she opened her eyes and was startled by my presence. The violin slipped from her fingers, but I sprang from the chair and caught it before it crashed to the floor. I carefully handed it back to her.

"You give forth a sound that is pleasing to my ears and a visage that is pleasing to my eyes," I told her, causing her to blush. "May I have the honor of knowing your name?"

"Anna," she said simply.

I bowed my head to her. "I am pleased to meet you, Anna. I am Kieran of Sungrove."

"Sungrove? I have never heard of such a place. Is it beyond the sea?" she asked in wonderment.

Her liveliness made me smile. "Yes, it is," I answered. "Maybe I can tell you about it sometime, but for now, I would like you to teach me how to play the violin as you do."

She seemed excited that I was interested in music and opened another violin case. She handed me a violin and bow. "Can you keep up?" she asked playfully.

"I don't think I'll have a problem," I answered with a laugh.

We raised the instruments to our chins and rested the bows on the strings. She began playing the song that led me here. Her intonation was very precise, suggesting that she had been playing for many years. I watched for a moment before falling in time with her, and she was impressed that I really was able to keep up. We forgot the world around us as we swayed together with the intoxicating music.

This girl had definitely captured my attention, but I didn't want to drink her thoughts to know everything about her. I wanted to savor each moment with her and build a lasting relationship.

We finished the piece, and she congratulated me. "Wow! That was amazing!" She put the violins back in their cases. "So how long have you been playing?"

I couldn't tell her that it was my first time, but I didn't want to lie to her either. "I've played the guitar for many years, so it wasn't hard to pick up the violin. What about you?"

She offered me a seat, and we both sat down. "I started taking lessons when I was nine," she answered. "I was a bit of a loner growing up, so my parents helped me find a hobby."

"Where are your parents now, if you don't mind me asking?"

"They still live in Connecticut. I moved here about a year ago to get a job at the Buffalo Zoological Gardens. My parents took me to the zoo when I was little, and I absolutely loved it."

"It sounds like you do," I commented. Seeing her smile made me smile. She was so charming. "What is your favorite animal?"

"Definitely the lions. To hear them roar, it's like it resonates within you. You admire and fear them at the same time." A look of shock came over her. "Oh, I have to go to work in a few hours. I need to get some sleep."

We both stood, and she led me to the door.

"I'm sorry to have kept you up at this late hour," I apologized.

"Don't be sorry. It was nice having company." As she opened the door for me to leave, she seemed confused for a moment. "I thought I had locked this door. How did you get in?"

"I heard music coming from within and had to know who was playing the violin so beautifully. I didn't want to interrupt your playing if I didn't have to, so I tried the knob, and the door simply opened. I am sorry for the intrusion, but I just had to—"

With a smile, she held her hand up to stop me. "Like I said, don't be sorry. And you are a fellow musician," she added with exuberance. "We should get together and play again sometime."

"Yes," I agreed. "I would like that very much." I stepped down onto the sidewalk and looked up to her. She was a lovely young lady about the age of 19. Standing at a slim 5'2", she had long, silky dark hair and dark, alluring eyes.

"I finish work at five tomorrow. If you like, stop by, and I will give you a personal tour of the zoo."

"Okay," I told her with a smile. "I will be there."

"All right then, I will see you tomorrow. Goodnight, Kieran of Sungrove."

"Goodnight, Anna of Connecticut," I said with a bow before she slowly closed the door.

I walked down the city sidewalk with a warm feeling of happiness that I hadn't felt in ages. My mind raced with things I should and shouldn't do to keep my identity a secret. I supposed I should pick up some fresh clothes before going to the zoo the following day.

There would still be daylight when I got there, so I would have to wear a cloak. I would just have to tell Anna that my skin is sensitive to the sun. While I was there, I looked into getting a place to live, so I could fit in a little better and have somewhere to stay. I couldn't wait to see Anna again.

CHAPTER XIV

RELIGIOUS DIFFERENCES

Our carriage arrived at Anna's Connecticut home. It had been nearly two years since we first met, and she was taking me to meet her parents for the first time. Anna said this will be the last time that we will be together in our frail, mortal bodies, so we were spending the last few hours with her parents. I wanted to laugh, but who was I to say that she was wrong? I didn't even know if my own religion was true. She had been talking about this for months, so if nothing happened at midnight, I planned to tell her everything and offer her immortality.

While living amongst humans, I had learned that an alarming number of them believed that a bearded man named Jesus would return at dawn of the twentieth century to take all those who believed he exists into Heaven. I had heard of the Christian God centuries ago, but only recently had I heard people would be raptured on New Year's Day.

They describe Heaven as a spirit realm in the atmosphere surrounding the planet where everyone lives in a palace and looks down upon the living. It's funny how similar it is to the elves' description of the Sun.

Our driver opened the door for us, and I helped Anna down the small carriage steps. We were both well-dressed beneath our full length coats, and she was stunningly gorgeous in her fur lined hat. I checked my pocket watch and saw that we had less than four hours until midnight. I tied my hair back with a ribbon, and we followed a stone walkway across the lawn to the large, two-story Colonial house. Light emitted from every window, and human shapes could be seen moving within.

As we walked, I purposely bumped into her to make her laugh. She giggled and then bumped into me. We continued to laugh and play as we walked. She stepped too close to the edge of the walkway and lost her balance. I grabbed hold and pulled her into my arms. Our laughter stopped as she stared at me with those big, brown eyes.

"I could lose myself forever in your eyes," I whispered.

"Well, shut up and get lost already," she said with a grin, and I closed the distance between our lips.

We stepped onto the porch her parent's house. We could hear talking and laughter inside. Anna tapped the door knocker three times. We looked at each other and shared a smile. The warmth of her kiss still lingered on my lips. The door opened, and a distinguished gentleman looked out at us with a big smile on his face. I could tell right away that he was Anna's father.

"Papa!" Anna said excitedly.

"Anna!" he said, hugging her. He was so glad to see his little girl again. "How is Buffalo?"

Anna's mother saw us and quickly made her way over to welcome us.

"It's great," she answered, but I could tell she was glad to be home. She pulled away from him and hugged her mother.

"My dear, sweet girl," her mother said.

"I've missed you so much," Anna told her.

"Good evening, young man," her father said to me, shaking my hand. "Beth," he called, turning to his wife, "we gotta get this boy inside; his hands are deathly cold."

"Good evening to you, sir," I responded with a chuckle.

"You must be Kieran," he continued. "I'm Samuel, and this is my wife, Bethany."

Bethany kissed me on the cheek. "Hello Kieran. Yes, we are so glad you could finally come. We have been so anxious to meet you."

Samuel laughed at his wife's excitement. A cold breeze caused him to shiver. "Beth, it's December. Don't you think it's a bit cold out here?"

"Oh yes. I'm sorry," she apologized. "Come inside. Come inside. We have plenty to eat."

". . . And plenty to drink!" Samuel added with a big laugh.

We all laughed as we stepped out of the cold. The house was full of people conversing with one another. Everyone was well-dressed and drinking wine.

"Kieran, would you like something to drink?" Bethany asked as she poured herself a glass of red wine.

I held back a bit of laughter. If only she knew. "No, thank you," I answered. "Maybe later," thinking that I could drink from her and see Anna growing up through her mother's eyes.

"Well, whenever you're ready, just help yourself."

"Thank you. I will," I said with a smile, loving the wordplay that she was unaware of.

A lady came over and started talking to her. I turned my attention to Anna, who was making her way around to speak to everyone. It seemed her entire family was here to await the coming of Jesus.

Samuel saw me standing alone and walked over. He handed me a glass of wine. I took it out of politeness, but I didn't drink.

"Just think, Kieran," he began, looking out at his family. "This time tomorrow, we will be having another party like this one, only we will be in Heaven."

I didn't say anything. I watched Anna, from across the room, stoop over to give a hug to her grandmother who was sitting in a big, comfortable chair in front of the fireplace. She then took a seat next to her, holding her hand as they talked. I focused to hear her grandmother say that she couldn't wait to see grandpa again. I began remembering my own family and the things that had happened. As time went by, I doubted more and more that our spirit flies into the Sun when we die. It was good that these people held so much faith in their beliefs. I hoped Jesus would return that night. Even if he didn't return for me, that would at least rekindle the hope that my family is waiting for me in the afterlife. A hand on my shoulder brought me out of my thoughts, and my ears were once again flooded by all the noise in the house.

"You two have been courting for quite some time now, haven't you?" Samuel asked as he watched his daughter.

"Yes sir," I answered. "Going on two years now."

"She told me how you two met," he continued. "God must have brought you together so you wouldn't have to be alone when his son returns to take us home. Anna had always preferred independence to companionship until she met you." He took a sip of his wine. "Everything happens for a reason, Kieran. Everything happens for a reason."

Samuel really caught my attention with that last statement. "What do you mean?" I asked him.

He took another sip of his wine, savoring the taste before answering. "God has a plan for us all."

"So you're saying that nothing happens by chance and that we are not in control of our actions?"

He raised his glass and began to speak in a glorious tone. "We are but actors in a grand play which He alone holds the script."

"So does this grand play end at midnight?" I asked him, now interested in the Christian religion.

"No," he answered. "We begin Act Two." He then turned up his glass to drink the last of it.

As Anna talked with her grandmother, she gave me a warm smile. She then excused herself and walked over to me. She kissed me on the cheek and caressed my face. "Excuse me, papa, but you can't keep him all to yourself," she said as she took hold of my hand and pulled me away.

"I'm sorry, dear," he said with a laugh. "Introduce him to the family."

Anna led me around to meet her family. Everyone was having a good time sharing stories and laughs.

A few minutes before midnight, Samuel interrupted. "Everyone, it is almost time. Let's all go outside and watch the sky for His return."

Everyone walked out into the cold, night air and into the large, front yard. Most didn't even wear a coat as they believed they would not feel cold for very long.

I led Anna to the side of the house where no one could see us. "Where are you taking me?" she asked playfully, thinking I wanted some alone time to shower her with kisses during our end moments.

"I have a secret that I want to share with you," I answered. "Close your eyes," and she did. I took her in my arms and leaped straight up to the top of her parent's house. "Open your eyes, my love."

Anna opened her eyes, and her face lit up with amazement as she realized where we were. The house had a flat roof that was only accessible from the inside, so she wondered how we got up there so quickly.

I kissed her cheek and pulled her face around to kiss her lips. "We have been together for quite some time now," I began. "We are friends. We are lovers. We are companions. We have been sharing our lives with one another, but there is a side of me that I haven't shared with you."

Anna looked at me with a questioning face.

"I am not as young as I appear to be," I continued. "I know this will come as a shock to you, but please try to stay calm. I am actually 1,638 years old."

She began to laugh. "What?"

"I am not human," I told her, letting my ears take their natural shape.

Anna stopped laughing. She covered her mouth and backed away from me.

"I am an elf," I finally admitted, "and the reason why I have grown to be so old, and still appear so young, is because I am a vampire."

"Vampire," she whispered to herself. "Why are you telling me this?"

"I am telling you this because I want to share my immortal existence with you."

"Immortal existence," she repeated, raising her voice. "I'm not staying. The Lord Jesus Christ will be here at the stroke of midnight to take his followers home."

I took out my pocket watch and held it up for her to see. "It's already three minutes after," I told her disappointedly. "He's not coming."

She snatched the watch from my hand and held it in the moonlight to see for herself. Angrily, she threw it at my chest. I didn't try to catch it. I just let it hit me and hang from the chain attached to my lapel.

She walked over to the guard railing at the edge of the roof. She saw her family standing in the road, holding candles, and looking up at the clear night sky.

"Come with me, Anna."

She took a deep breath and turned to face me. She slowly approached and ran a finger along the edge of one of my ears. "This isn't a dream, is it?" she asked, already knowing the answer.

"No," I assured her. "It's not a dream. I have the power to give you eternal life. Your body will not wrinkle with age. You can be as you are now, forever. Will you accept?"

Tears welled up in her eyes. "No," she answered, turning away from me. She looked up into the sky and wiped the tears from her face.

We were both quiet for a long moment. She looked out over the railing again and saw her family blowing out their candles as they walked back toward the house.

"Anna, I'm still the same person I was yesterday," I explained. "Didn't you love me yesterday?" I waited for her to answer, but she didn't. "Please say something."

She turned quickly to face me. "What do you want me to say?" she snapped. "What am I supposed to say? You've been lying to me all this time! You've led me to believe that you are the most wonderful man that I could ever know. Now you tell me that you are a vampire. A vampire, Kieran! You are a demon in physical form. You are an evil spirit that has claimed the body of one who once lived."

"No," I fired back. "I am not a demon. Believe me, I have wanted to tell you since the day I first laid eyes on you. I didn't because I hoped, by the time I did tell you, you would love me enough to not be frightened by me."

"How can I believe anything that you say

now?" she asked with a venomous tone. She walked to the opposite side of the roof where a door was built up from the inside staircase.

I heard her try to open the door. "It's locked," I said without looking at her.

"I want to go back inside," she told me with her back to me. "We're finished, Kieran."

I turned to see her standing in front of the door with her head down. "Anna," I said soothingly, "think rationally for one moment. You said that you believed me to be the most wonderful man that you could ever know." I slowly walked over to her. "What is different now, other than knowing my age, to make you believe otherwise?"

Just as I was about to lay my hands on her shoulders, she turned to face me. "You drink from the living, do you not?" her words strong and direct.

I took a deep breath, for I feared that she was truly lost to me. I reluctantly answered, "I drink blood, yes, but I am not dead. I am more alive than you can imagine."

With the same strong, unfaltering tone, she asked, "And you want me to be like you?"

"I offer you this because I love you, Anna." My words weighed heavy with emotion. I stroked her cheek with the back of my fingers. "I cannot bear to watch you grow old and die."

She closed her eyes for a moment, remembering the love we shared. She then took my hand away from her face. "Death is the price for living," she explained.

I shook my head. "It doesn't have to be. We can be—"

"I look forward to the day I see my grandpa again," she cut me off. Tears began to well up in her eyes as she remembered him. "What about God?" she continued, choked up through the tears. "Must I shun God so I may feed upon his sheep?"

"I know no god," I admitted coldly.

Anna was shocked by my answer. She couldn't even begin to imagine the losses I had endured, and here she was condemning me. I wanted to believe, I really did. I hoped that the Christian God would bathe the Earth in an inescapable light to cleanse it of all life. I wanted my body to be destroyed, to release my spirit from this immortal shell so that I may fly into the Sun. Now the hope I hold that there is an afterlife hangs by a failing thread.

Tears streamed down her face as she whispered a prayer: "Forgive me, Lord, for falling under the spell of this demon. Give me the strength to resist his power."

"I can assure you that I have never used my powers to charm you or to read your thoughts."

"This is a test!" she assumed. A smile broke across her face. "God must be testing my faith. Know that I will not falter," she said with renewed strength. "I don't want to see you anymore, Kieran." Even in her coat, she shivered in the cold, night air. She wiped the tears from her face again and crossed her arms tight around her chest.

"Very well," I said sadly. I reached past her and took hold of the door knob. I magically released the lock and opened the door for her. The warm air rushed out to ease our winter chill.

"I am going to spend a few days here with my

family." She stepped inside, holding the door open to speak to me. "It's time for you to leave."

A single tear streamed down my face. "Anna, look at this from every angle before you make a decision," I pleaded.

For the first time, she saw me cry tears of blood, and she was disturbed by it. "I have made my decision," she told me in a tone as bitter as the cold. She closed the door and locked it.

I heard her sniffling on the other side of the door, and then she slowly walked down the stairs to rejoin her family.

I used a handkerchief to wipe the tears from my face. I was once again alone. I dropped down from the roof and followed the road to the city.

CHAPTER XV

A HARD LESSON

It was a bright, summer day in New York. I was sitting on a bench, shaded by buildings. My cloak was draped over the iron arm of the bench, and I used a spell to hide my ears. From where I was sitting, I could see Anna with her husband and their young son having lunch at an outside diner. She seemed very happy.

"Why do you do this to yourself?" a voice asked from next to me.

I turned my head quickly to see Manius sitting beside me. I hadn't sensed anyone was near.

"It's self-torture," he continued.

I didn't say anything. I turned to look back at Anna.

"You want her don't you?" he asked, already knowing the answer.

"Very much," I answered without looking away

from her.

"Then take her," he emphasized. "Give her immortality."

"No. I cannot turn her against her will."

Manius laid a hand on my shoulder. "You truly are a good person, and I love you for that, but you shouldn't torture yourself like this," he said, seeing the pain within me.

"I know," I admitted, turning my gaze to the asphalt beneath my feet.

"I suggest you let her live her life, and ask her again at the end of it."

That wasn't a bad idea. Maybe she would think differently when she was on death's doorstep. Looking back at Manius, "Will my blood make her young again?"

Manius thought for a moment. "I'm not for certain she will return to the age that you two met, but your blood will certainly heal her of the frailties of old age."

"What if she still refuses?"

"Then do what you feel is right," he answered simply. "I trust you will do what is best."

I turned my attention to Anna. "What if something happens to her before I come back?"

Manius stood from his seat next to me. "Then it will be no different from her telling you no."

I threw my cloak over my shoulder, and we walked down the shaded sidewalk.

To someone like me, 45 years is nothing, and now I came to give Anna one last chance for eternal life. I hoped she would accept this time.

It was late afternoon, and I walked down a sidewalk in Jersey to the house where she was living out her retirement. I took hold of the doorknob and listened for a moment before walking in. I heard only one heart beating from inside. I silently entered the house and found a gray-haired lady sitting with her back to me in front of a gas fireplace. I was hesitant to see Anna again after all those years, but I finally walked around to the side of the chair to look at her.

By the light of an electric lamp, she read her Bible and didn't notice me standing next to her. I was saddened that she had grown old and feeble. She was no longer the fresh, young beauty that she once was.

I looked around to see a statue of the Virgin Mary on the mantle and other religious artifacts throughout the room. There were also family pictures along the mantle and cluttered on the tables. She had a beautiful family with three children. I imagined her husband had already passed on, but it appeared that she lived a rich, full life.

I looked back at Anna and remembered how she used to be, how we used to be. We took many afternoon strolls through the zoo. We wrote wonderful pieces of music together. We spent many a night looking up at the stars from the rooftop. She got used to the fact that my skin was sensitive to the sun and that I didn't like anyone to see me eat. I remembered her saying that my oddities were what made me unique, and she kissed me on the nose. Of course, she was unaware that was how the elves used to show affection for one another.

Memories of Tess began to surface. Oh, how I

loved her. I would give every ounce of my blood to have her back. The same goes for Kelena and the rest of my family. I miss them so much. A single crimson tear fell down my face to bring me from my thoughts.

Anna was still focused on her Bible. I believe I was attracted to her because she reminded me of Tess, and I wanted her to fill that void in my life. I was wrong to think that she could. I looked at her one last time before I slowly backed out of the room and walked outside. I closed the door gently to not alarm her.

It began to drizzle as I walked down the sidewalk. The street lamps looked like stars that went on forever into the night. I was still quite a way from my New York apartment, and the rain was getting heavy, but I didn't care. I could teleport home in a flash, but the rain was refreshing. I walked for miles before finally taking a seat on a bench. I laid my head back and closed my eyes, letting the rain shower me.

The world is unrecognizable from the one in my memories. Trees have been replaced with skyscrapers. Grass had been paved over with asphalt. Horses have been surpassed by the automobile. No, this is not the world I remember. This is the world of man, a world that I feel I can never truly be a part of.

Since the prophecy of Jesus' return did not occur, I began to wonder why we even believe in an afterlife. How do we know the stories we hear are true? What if there is nothing after death? What if the hope of eternal happiness is only to prepare mortals for their inevitable end? They breathe their last breath believing they are going to meet all those who died before them when, in actuality, their memories fade, and their conscious mind loses all sense of anything ever existing.

If my sister had died in the forest with Tess, would I have still accepted immortality, or would I have wished for death? Would I risk facing the nothingness for the hope of seeing my family again? At the time, I probably would have chosen death; I had no doubts that I would ascend to the Sun. Now I need more than hope; I need proof that death isn't the end.

I sensed a man approaching, but I did not open my eyes to look. He was walking casually down the sidewalk toward me. It was Manius. He took a seat but I did not acknowledge his presence.

"It's almost unbearable, the loss of all who we have known and loved," he said to me, "but that is the price we pay for immortality. People live and die, yet we stay the same. A lifetime to them seems but a day to us, and we are left carrying the sorrow of all who have passed on."

I finally raised my head and opened my eyes to look at him. He was very well-dressed and completely dry. Even in the midst of this downpour, the rain didn't seem to touch him.

"You may not believe me," he continued, "but I have always held great admiration for you. I admire your courage against unbelievable odds, and I admire your respect for mortal life. I know you didn't ask for immortality, but that's what makes you who you are. Someone who seeks immortality seeks it because they fear death. They do not want to die. They are afraid that, once they reach the end of their life, they simply cease to exist, and most care nothing of others. But you, you are different."

I stared into the light of one of the street lamps. "I once believed that the Sun contained the spirits of the dead, and the stars contained the spirits from other worlds. Now, since I've walked the Earth and observed many cultures, I question my faith. I wish I could see for myself if spirits really do reside there. With so many religions and beliefs in the world, how can I say that I am right if I haven't seen for myself that it is the truth?"

"And that is why you show great respect for mortal life," Manius pointed out. "You know they will live their lives and then see what lies beyond it. You think that, because you are immortal, you may never know if your loved ones are waiting for you to join them in the afterlife, or if there is an afterlife at all."

"What secrets do you believe death holds?" I asked. "Do you believe our consciousness moves on after the body dies?"

"We both have seen death when we were made vampires," he told me.

I looked away, remembering the night Sylvia and I fed on one another. "My body was overtaken with paralysis, and then I blacked out."

"And that, my friend, is Death's grip," Manius said, closing his fingers into a fist.

"Well, what about the spirit?" I continued to question. "Do you believe, if our bodies are destroyed, our spirit will be released to whatever afterlife?"

He took a moment to gather his thoughts. "Personally, I don't believe that we are spirits working through flesh. If we were, then why did you black out? What purpose is there for a spirit to lose consciousness with the body? I do, however, believe that there is more to reality than we can comprehend. So even if there is nothing beyond life, that doesn't mean we can't make the best of what we have."

The rain stopped, taking our attention away from our conversation. Manius placed a hand on my shoulder, and I began to dry. I watched the rain water leave me as steam.

"I'm glad you're here," I told him with a smile. "Thank you."

"You are truly welcome," Manius said, returning the smile. He stood from the bench. "Walk with me."

I stood, and we walked quietly down the empty sidewalk, taking in the peacefulness of the night and the freshness of the air. We began crossing a long bridge, and we stopped about midway to look out over the river.

Manius finally spoke. "So you decided against making Anna a vampire."

"Yes," I hesitantly confirmed. "I realized that I had been using her in an attempt to fill the void of a lost loved one."

"You mean the void left by the loss of Tess?" he asked, a genuine sadness coming through in his voice.

I answered with only a nod.

"I saw visions of her and felt the love you hold for her when I drank from you in Byron's temple. I know that is why you keep your distance from everyone now. I understand. You have lost everything, everything but yourself, and you have chosen solitude to acquiring and losing more loved ones. Well, I want you to know that I am here for you if you need anything. I am here for you if you need someone to talk to. I know all too well how it feels to be alone. As you already know, I am not an ancient Red Dragon as I pretended to be long ago, but what you don't know is that I am the first of our kind of vampire."

My sadness turned to amazement. "The first?" I asked. "How could you keep that secret for so long?"

"I have kept my identity secret by blocking my thoughts from others to read," he explained. "I led everyone to believe that I was the eldest of the Red Dragons, so I could hold a position on the World Council. I used a spell that I had learned from a powerful wizard to give me the abilities."

"That's how you survived the lava within the Earth," I said, voicing my thoughts.

"Yes."

"Why would you want to do this?" I asked. "Why go through all the trouble?"

"As a member of the council, I could voice my opinion on how I believe the world should be shaped. I did all this to protect the human race because I am human. I was the only one who had the power to stand up for them, so I did."

"And you kept this a secret from everyone all this time," I voiced my thoughts again, completely amazed. "That's incredible, but how did you become a vampire?"

"I was born in 2376 BC in Crete," Manius began. "I lived a full life like any other, but during the winter of 2322, I fell greatly ill. I was sure I would be fine because I was never sick for more than a week, but I was quite old now and not the man I once was." Lost in thought, he seemed sad, remembering his final days. "The sickness became worse, and I was bed ridden. As I was breathing my last breaths, my longtime friend and companion, Vistilia told me to make a wish. I told her, 'I want us to be rid of these old and feeble bodies. We should be young and strong forever.' She kissed me, and I died. I awoke in a crypt where Vistilia was waiting for me. We both looked like we were once again in the prime of our lives. She told me what she had done to me and the limitations that she added along with my wish. She explained that the limitations can be overcome, but they were needed to challenge me, to give me a personal perfection to reach for. I also found that I had a burning hunger like no other."

A spark of hope shone in my eyes. "So our limitations can be surpassed, and one day, I may be able to watch the sunrise again?"

Manius smiled at my childlike excitement. "Overcoming our sensitivity to sunlight is insignificant to the power that we can possess."

"How do I attain this power?" I asked him, hardly able to contain myself.

"Like our lives so far, I believe it is a gradual process of learning and growing mentally as well as physically. It is only a matter of time, my friend."

"What was the purpose of creating us? Why did Vistilia choose you?"

Manius sighed heavily. "At first, I believed she truly loved me and didn't want me to die, but then, when she left, I wasn't sure. I remembered that I had known her my entire life. It's as if she had already chosen me."

"Why did she leave?" I asked curiously.

Manius stared off at the waters of the Hudson. "She wanted me to grow on my own. She wanted me to learn without her aid. She didn't tell me when she would return. She only said, 'A millennium to you is but a moment to me.'" He then went quiet.

"Wait. There must be more to this story," I told him, eager to learn the reason of it all. "Tell me everything. I want to hear it all."

He turned to face me, and I saw his eyes were glazed in red, and a blood tear had fallen down his cheek. It seemed that Vistilia left him like Sylvia left me. "You truly loved her, didn't you?"

"More than life itself," he answered, his words thick with sadness. He wiped the tear away and looked at the crimson stain on his fingers. "It has been ages since I've shed a tear." He closed it into his fist.

The darkness began to fade with the coming dawn.

"I'm glad you're interested in my story. I have kept it secret for far too long. I still have much to tell you, but we have all the time in the world." He put a hand on my shoulder, and we made our way toward New York. "Let's get us a bite," he said with a smile.

We ran the rest of the way across the bridge and into the city. The few people that were already out that morning didn't notice us because we passed by so quickly. I followed Manius into an alleyway between two apartment buildings.

"Listen," he said, looking up at the many windows along the brick building. "Can you hear them sleeping?"

I focused and began hearing slow deep breaths coming from all around me. "Yes," I whispered. "I can hear them."

He looked to a window three floors up and said, "Let's take that one." He grabbed my wrist, and in a flash, we were standing inside the apartment. I could immediately tell a man lived there because the place could use a good cleaning; that and the pair of men's shoes on the floor next to the ugly, ogre shit-green sofa.

I followed Manius into the bedroom and found a man in his mid-twenties asleep with a young woman. Manius walked around the bed to the young man. He pushed the pin on his alarm clock so it wouldn't go off. He stared at each of them for a moment. *"Can you see their dreams?"* he asked telepathically so he wouldn't wake them.

I stared at the couple but saw nothing. I shook my head.

"Try closing your eyes," he suggested. *"Reach out with your thoughts to see with your third eye. Once you get a clear picture of your surroundings, focus on the woman, and reach into her mind."*

I tried again, doing as Manius suggested. With my eyes closed, I got a mental image of the room. I then looked into the woman's dream. It was hazy, but I could tell she was afraid of something. She was running away. She was running from another man. I looked deeper, past the dream. The images became clearer, and I saw memories of her with the man in her dreams. It was her husband. She was having an affair and was afraid she would get caught. I pulled away, returning to the visual world.

Manius was smiling. He knew that I saw. *"Now look at the young man's dream,"* he told me as if he knew something.

I closed my eyes and reached out with my mind to the sleeping, young man. I looked into the haze of his dream. I saw him struggling, but what was he struggling against? Beyond the veil of his dream, I saw the woman. The two worked third shift in a factory but had skipped work to be together. He found bruises on her back where her husband beat her. The young man had begged her to go to the police, but she wouldn't. She was afraid. She said that he wouldn't be locked away forever, and then he would come for her. Her young lover had bought a gun. He had it hidden in a shoe box in the closet. He was planning to kill her husband! I had seen enough. I stopped reading his thoughts and looked at Manius. *"What should we do?"* I asked him.

"I think we should pay her husband a visit," he answered with a mischievous smile. *"But first, we can't let our breakfast go to waste. It is the most important meal of the day, you know."* We quietly laughed, and I saw his canines extend. He then bit into the man's neck.

I walked around to the woman and sank my teeth into her. As I drank, I retrieved a vision of her home, so we could pay her husband a little visit. When I finished, I bit my tongue and licked the two small punctures on her neck. My blood instantly healed her wounds to hide that she was bitten. I turned to find Manius observing me, and I suddenly felt a bit shy. I was not used to having someone watch me drink. *"I know where she lives,"* I told him so that we could move on. *"Are we ready to slay another monster?"*

He shook his head. He took hold of my wrist

and teleported us back into the alleyway. "You never read Anna's mind, did you?" he asked me bluntly.

I was taken off guard by his question, but I answered him. "No, I didn't. Why?"

"Don't get me wrong, she was a wonderful woman," he tried to put me at ease. "It's just that everyone has a point of view, and sometimes it can't easily be seen."

I pressed my lips together, not wishing to talk about this.

He saw that I was getting annoyed. "I'm sorry," he apologized. "I'm merely saying you could have saved yourself a lot of heartache if you had read her mind before getting attached."

"Are we ready to go?" I repeated, a bit agitated. He outstretched a hand. I took his wrist, and he teleported us to the woman's home.

We appeared in the living room of a house back in Jersey. The woman's husband was awake! He was standing over the stove in his white underwear as he boiled water to make instant coffee. He scraped the bottom of the can to spoon out just enough for a cup.

"*Don't move,*" Manius commanded of me.

"*Are you crazy?*" I telepathically yelled. "*We're standing in the middle of his living room! He'll see us!*" I struggled to move, but he had hold of me.

"*No, he won't,*" Manius assured me. "*Just be still.*"

The man took a sip of his coffee and walked over to the front door, opened it, and picked up a newspaper lying on the door step. He brought his coffee and newspaper into the living room and sat down on the sofa. He didn't see us!

I raised my hand but could not see it. I could only see what little heat my body was emitting. I turned to look at Manius, and he was invisible too. All I could see was his heat signature.

"*I picked up this little trick from the naga in Byron's temple,*" he admitted. "*What did you get from yours?*" he asked, a smile spreading across the aura of heat that I saw of him.

He extended his hand to the man on the sofa, but we were standing too far away to touch him. The man appeared to be getting sleepy. He sat his mug on the coffee table and yawned. His eyes were getting heavy, and his head began to nod. He laid his head back and quickly fell asleep. Manius released me, and we became visible.

"*So how are we going to handle this?*" I asked. "*We're not going to incinerate him, are we?*"

He laughed a little and spoke in a low tone, "This one here is a heavy sleeper."

I looked at the man to double-check that he was indeed sleeping and not dead. He was breathing. He was alive.

"Do you remember what I told you about point of view?" Manius asked with a sly grin. With a nod of his head toward the nearly nude wife beater, he said, "Take a look at our pasty friend's memories. See what makes him tick."

I looked at the man and entered his mind. There was no dream because he had just fallen asleep. I continued on, looking deeper. Like his wife, he was also a factory worker, but he hated his job. He wanted to move far away from the city, where he could breathe the open air, but his wife wanted to stay. He felt trapped, and his emotional state had reached a level where he physically abused her. He loved her, but the little things pushed him over the edge. I pulled away from him and turned to Manius. "He hates his life and takes his anger out on his wife," I whispered. "How can we help these people? If he stays, he will be murdered or end up in jail. But how do we get him to leave everything behind without revealing ourselves?"

"Observe," Manius said with a smile as he cracked his knuckles for dramatic effect. He closed his eyes for a moment, and then he grabbed my arm to turn us invisible again.

The man awakened and went into his bedroom. We followed him to see what he does. He threw a suitcase on the bed and began filling it with clothes. He got dressed, left his wedding ring on the night stand, and walked out.

Manius and I became visible. "What did you do?" I asked, looking out the window and laughing at how simple it seemed.

The man got in his car and drove away.

Manius picked up a pack of cigarettes that were lying on the kitchen table and tapped one out. He placed the cigarette between his lips, and with a snap of his fingers, it lit. He kicked back on the sofa and took a long draw before answering. "Not only can we read thoughts, we can implant them. To him, I seemed like his own conscience, formulating a plan to better his life." He took another draw from his cigarette. "I reminded him that he was unhappy and that he needed to do something now, or he could be here for the rest of his life. I told him that his wife will never leave the city and that she is holding him back from his dreams.

I suggested that he move to Texas and restart his life while he is still young."

"And that was it?" I asked, amazed. I took a seat in an adjacent chair.

"Well," he began, taking a draw from his cigarette. "I may have done more than suggest." He put out his cigarette in a nearby ashtray. "To someone with no knowledge of the arcane, we can make a tough decision seem like their only choice."

Sensing him leading into another conversation about my love life, I cut him off. "Manius, I don't want to talk about my failure with Anna."

He turned, put his feet on the floor, and clasped his hands together. "This is no longer about Anna. This is about everyone you will meet from this day forth. A person can spend a lifetime getting to know someone. We may have the luxury of time on our side, but there are still way too many people in the world for us to waste it on."

I may not have wanted to talk about it, but I understood what he was telling me. I nodded my head in agreement.

"Speaking of which," Manius said, standing, "I have some things to tend to in D.C."

I stood with him. "All right. The lady of the house should be arriving at any moment, so I guess it's time for us to leave."

"It's good seeing you again, Kieran." He began to shake my hand but then pulled me in for a hug. "If you need anything, just come to Lafayette Park and call my name. I'll see you again soon, my friend." He took a couple of steps back as he prepared to teleport away.

"Yes, thank you," I told him with a bow of my head. Then he was gone.

"Where to now?" I asked myself aloud. "I think I've had my feel of New York and Jersey. I think I'll go to my home in the Virginia Mountains and then venture south."

I was about to teleport home when I heard a car pull up in the driveway. I peeked out the window and saw the young man from New York sitting in his car. He had come alone. I reached out to read his thoughts. The woman was out buying groceries. He had come to kill her husband! He saw that his car was gone and suspected that he had already left for work. He backed out and drove away.

"It's a good thing Manius persuaded the man to leave. I just hope he treats his next wife a little better. I'm sure his first won't have any trouble filing for divorce now that he has left her. It looks like everything will be all right," I said with a bit of pride before teleporting home.

END

ACT I

CHAPTER XVI

KEVIN'S DREAMS

It was 12:17 A.M. Friday morning, and I was driving up at my parent's house. I had switched to a second shift position at my job, but I still hated it. I was tired of going to the same place to do the same thing eight hours a day, forty hours a week. How can people work the same job for twenty or more years? I had been there for nearly five, and I already felt like a zombie, dragging myself through a pitiful existence of making boxes, and for what? It's not like I was getting rich. I could work there until I retire and still have nothing, but what could I do? Even if I moved away, what was I going to do for money? I could hate working there just as much as I did here.

Ever since my band Visionary broke up, I've felt lost. My drummer and I were planning to move to the beach, but he found another band to play in. I wasn't sure why he ditched me. We don't exactly talk anymore. I tried forming another band, Beyond Illusion. I got another great drummer, a clever bassist, and a creative rhythm guitarist. We were in the process of finding a singer when the band fizzled out, and we went our separate ways. I wound up recording all the music myself, so I wouldn't forget it. I wasn't sure what to do. Perhaps I would take Kieran up on his offer.

It had been four years since I met him. He had offered me immortality, but I needed time to be sure of my decision. I have introduced him to my family, but of course, he magically conceals his pointy ears. They also didn't know that he came over to hang out as often as he did. I have several guitars, so we normally worked on music. Whenever my brother was here for the weekend, we liked to play video games.

My mom and step-dad had long since gone to bed, so I quietly made my way up the stairs. I opened my bedroom door to find Kieran sitting at my computer.

"Have a bad day?" he asked without taking his eyes off the screen. He was reading news on the Internet.

I breathed in deeply to relax myself as I took my shoes and socks off, leaving them by the door. I walked across the thick brown carpet to the window and looked out at the night sky. The carpet was soothing after spending eight hours walking on concrete. "I feel like I don't belong here," I told him, "but I've always felt this way. I am too different from everyone else."

I saw from the reflection in the window, Kieran

swivel around in my chair to look at me. "You have worked for so long to be different, to be your own person, that you feel you are too different now. You feel like you don't belong, but in reality, you don't want to belong."

I thought for a moment as it all became clear. "That's it." I turned from the window to look at him. "It all makes sense now. My entire life, I've been in my own little world. I may have played in a couple of bands, but I preferred solitude to parties. I guess that's why my bands broke up and why I have trouble finding a girlfriend."

"And that is why I chose you," Kieran explained. "I believe you can better handle the passing of time because you have already distanced yourself from the world."

"It wasn't a choice that came easily, believe me," I told him sadly. "And I still, at times, have trouble dealing with the loneliness."

"Well, that's understandable," he said, seeming like a shrink. "Feeling lonely is Nature's way of saying you should belong. You may feel stronger each time you resist Nature's charm, but she alienates you just a bit further."

"How did you find me?" I asked, sitting down on the bed. "I seem to have no secrets with you."

"I originally stopped in Seagrove because the name was similar to my own hometown. I began practicing my mind reading power, but instead of focusing on a single person's dream, I was reaching out to everyone around me. One particular dream stood out from the others," he said, holding up a finger. "It was a dream about vampires. I focused on this dream and followed it to its source to find an 8-year-old boy with his bed covers pulled up over his neck."

I was shocked that he had been watching me for ten years. "I remember!" I blurted out. "Well, I remember my nightmares. I don't remember you," I clarified.

Laughing a little, he continued his recollection of meeting me. "Every night, I watched terrifying dreams play out in your head, dreams not just of vampires but of werewolves, zombies, snakes, spiders, and witches. You often woke yourself up, frightened by the terrible visions. Other times, you would sleepwalk as you tried to escape your dreams, and your mother would put you back in your bed. You feared death. It seemed unnatural to me for someone so young to fear death as you did. Over the next few years, your dreams began to change; they no longer frightened you but excited you. You even daydreamed of going on fantastic quests to save people from monsters. You have always been a bit of a loner, but now you began to prefer fantasy to reality. Then one day, you thought to be a vampire might not be all that bad."

"I'm not quite sure why I became such a loner," I told him as I thought back on my life. "Maybe it was from growing up in the country and rarely having any kids my age to play with. Maybe it was from the disappointment of my friends moving on with their lives. Or maybe, it was from being a nobody in the eyes of the few girls that I've liked. Realizing that each new love in my life would rather be with someone else makes me just a little colder to the world."

"Until all you have left are your dreams,"

Kieran added.

Suddenly an idea struck me, and I looked at him with a glimmer of hope in my eyes. "You wouldn't happen to know any hot, elf women, would you?"

Kieran burst out laughing. "Believe me, if I knew some hot, elf women, we wouldn't be having this conversation."

Even though I was disappointed by the news, seeing him laugh made me laugh.

"So what's wrong with human women?" he asked.

I pressed my lips and twisted them in a quirky fashion as I thought for a second. "I just don't understand what goes on in their heads," I told him, pointing at my head.

"That can be said for every female, no matter their race."

"Why is that?" I asked. "Why is it that I think a girl is going to do one thing, but then she turns around and does something that makes completely no sense?"

"Because our brains work differently," he answered. "I've watched for centuries as men and women try and fail to understand each other. It's another one of Nature's tricks. Men and women are two halves of the whole. Men think logically where women think emotionally."

"So elf women are no different?"

"Nope. They are no different. They just stay hot ten times longer," Kieran answered with a smile.

"Hey, that counts for something."

We both laughed, and then he asked me, "What do you want to do with your life? You hate your job, and you don't care for being around a lot of people, so rock star may not be a good choice."

"Hmm, I don't know."

Kieran looked around my bedroom for ideas and noticed my collection of vampire books in my entertainment center. "Well, you like vampires, and you have a good imagination. What if you tried writing a book?"

I seemed to freeze up for a moment as I thought about making a living from storytelling. "That's a pretty good idea."

"Of course, you will have to work a regular job until you get your first book written, but you should have it easy after that."

"Yeah," I agreed, staring at my row of books. My imagination was already starting to kick into gear.

"What about retirement?" he asked, sending my mind farther into the future. "What would you like to do with your time after writing a few books?"

"I want to travel the universe," I answered, standing up to return to the window. "Like my Physical Science teacher always said: 'Space is the place.' Look out there," I told him. "There are about 300 billion stars in our galaxy alone, and there are countless galaxies. I want to visit other worlds. I want to communicate with intelligent life on other planets." I paused, thinking of all the studying that I had been doing so I could best him in our next religious discussion, but the more I read, the more he seemed right. "The people that say there is nothing out there," I continued, "don't realize how big the universe really is. This leads me to the conclusion that we are arrogant to believe, within the entire universe, we are the special ones made in the image of an all-powerful god."

Kieran sat quietly in my desk chair as he listened to me speak.

"Given enough time, human technology will have to advance enough to get me off this rock." I turned away from the window to face my friend. "I don't want to grow old waiting for a technology that may not come within my lifetime. I want to live forever," I told him, sure of my decision.

With only a nod, he was happy that I finally accepted eternal life.

"My mom and step-dad have beach reservations for the week of the fourth, and my brother is going with a few of his friends to stay in a beach house that same week." I sat down on the edge of the bed. "If your offer is still good, I think that will be the best time for me to um . . . make the transition."

"My offer is still good," he said with a smile. "I'm glad to hear that you're ready."

I yawned, reminding me that I was tired, and I glanced at my VCR clock to see that it was nearly three A.M. No wonder I was tired; I was usually in bed by two. Kieran was already shutting down the computer. He knew that I was tired.

"Kieran, I think it's about bedtime," I told him.

He stood, pushing my chair under the desk. "Well, have a good evening at work tomorrow."

"All right," I told him, standing up to make my way to the bathroom.

"I'll see you this weekend."

"Okay," I said sleepily.

Kieran vanished, teleporting to who knows

where.

      I walked through my brother's room to get to the bathroom. He wasn't there that night, so I didn't have to worry about waking him. Dad would bring him over after school Friday. I brushed my teeth and headed back to my room. Being sleepy, I clumsily stripped down to my undies, turned off my light, and got under the covers. My mind didn't buzz with thoughts. I only noticed the warmth of my bed and welcomed the fantastic dreams that came for me.

CHAPTER XVII

A BAD NIGHT

Kieran, my brother Neill, and I walked out of a mall after seeing a movie. My blond hair was very long and pulled back into a ponytail. Kieran also had his hair pulled back.

Neill looked at me and asked, "That one good enough to buy?" Meaning, when the movie was released on video, did I think it was good enough that I would buy it.

"Yep. That was awesome," I told him enthuse-astically. "What did you think, Kieran?"

Before he could answer, Dirk dropped out of nowhere! He shoved me away with both hands and kicked Kieran in the face. He telekinetically threw Neill into a lamp post, knocking him out.

Kieran quickly recovered. "Why have you returned?" he asked Dirk.

"I've come for you," he answered as they circled each other.

I got up and ran to attack Dirk. The three of us fought hand-to-hand until Dirk summoned a pair of kamas. Kieran summoned a pair of sais, and I, a katana.

We fought for a few moments more before a security guard saw what was going on and radioed for backup as he ran toward us. Within seconds, a mall security vehicle sped around the building. The S.U.V. slid to a stop, and two more security guards, a male and female, got out.

Without taking his eyes away from Dirk, Kieran yelled, "Stay out of this," to the guards.

Having no weapons, the security guards were not equipped to handle this kind of situation. "Stop fighting, and drop your weapons!" one guard commanded. "The police are on their way," he warned.

I blocked one of Dirk's attacks. Kieran backhanded a cut across his cheek with the tip of a sai. I then sliced Dirk above his left knee, and Kieran stabbed him in the belly. Losing his concentration, his weapons dispersed, and he doubled over. Before I could take his head, Dirk swung both of his hands out to telekinetically force me and Kieran away from him. He then threw the three security guards against their vehicle, knocking them out.

Dirk summoned another kama but whipped a long chain from it to create a kusarigama. Kieran threw a sai at his head, but he swung the ghastly weapon to block it. The sai exploded into a small burst of light.

The guard that was first on the scene picked himself up from the asphalt. Dirk gave me a smile and a wink as he swung the weighted end of the kusarigama toward the guard. I quickly intercepted and used my sword to block Dirk's weapon from its target. The chain wrapped around my katana, and he pulled in close. He sliced my throat with the blade of the weapon, and I lost my sword as I desperately grasped at my neck in an attempt to stop the bleeding.

Kieran lunged at him with a sai, but Dirk leaped straight up, disappearing into the night sky.

I fell to the ground, holding my throat. Blood was pooling around me. The guard grabbed a first aid kit from the S.U.V. and raced over to help.

"He is going into shock," the guard said to Kieran.

Kieran placed his left hand on my forehead. "Close your eyes. Control your breathing. Relax. You're not going anywhere."

The bleeding began to slow. The guard wiped some of the blood from my neck and wrapped gauze around it.

"I'll be right back," Kieran told me.

He checked Neill to make sure he was okay. "Just lie still for a moment," he told him.

Kieran then went to each security guard and placed a hand on their heads to erase the memory of what just happened. The guards woke up looking around as if lost for a moment. "Thank you for your help," Kieran told them. "I think we will be okay now."

The three security guards got in their vehicle and looked back to see me slowly getting to my feet. "Okay. We're glad we could help," the woman said, and they drove away.

I took my bandage off. My neck had almost completely healed. I staggered over to check on my brother.

Kieran ran over to help me walk. "Easy now. You're very weak from blood loss. You need to feed."

Neill sat up, rubbing the back of his head. "What happened?" he asked groggily.

"You passed out and fell into that lamp post," I told him. "Gave us a good scare. I think we need to get you home." Neill doesn't know that vampires truly exist, and I wasn't about to tell him that his brother was one, not that day anyway.

Kieran helped him to his feet, and we walked across the parking lot to my car. Feeling light-headed from the loss of blood, I let Kieran drive us home.

Being as late as it was when we got home, Neill went to bed. He didn't get hurt too badly, just a bump on the head and minor scrapes on his arms.

After closing my bedroom door, Kieran allowed me to drink from his wrist to regain my strength. We then climbed out my window to sit on the roof. It was a warm, summer night, and the thick rolling clouds suggested we would have thunder-showers soon.

"Dirk must be destroyed," he said, not turning his eyes away from the sky.

"So what are we going to do?" I asked him, prepared to do whatever was necessary.

He looked at me with a smile that thanked me for my bravery. "Not we," he corrected me, shaking his head. "I cannot risk losing you like I lost Kelena." He stood to leave.

"What?" I asked, standing up to stop him. "I

can help you. You need my help," I argued.

Kieran pulled me in for a hug. "I know, but I'm sorry."

"I don't want you to go alone," I stressed.

"I won't be. I'm going to D.C. to speak with Manius. He can help me."

I nodded my head in agreement. I didn't like this plan of him leaving to fight Dirk, but I believed Manius was the only one strong enough to help him. "Well, can you at least take me to D.C. with you?" I asked. "I've heard you talk about Manius, but I've never met him. Plus, I'd like to hear what he has to say about Dirk."

He thought for a moment, but I could already tell by the look on his face that he didn't like the idea.

"You can bring me back before you leave to find Dirk," I explained. "We're not going to be gone but maybe a couple of hours, right?"

"All right, but what if your parents come up looking for you?" he asked.

"I'll just leave a note at my bedroom door saying that I left with you and that I'll be back in a little while. I should be back before they wake up, though."

"All right. Write your note and we'll go," he told me.

I climbed through the window into my bedroom and pulled out a piece of printer paper from a pack on my computer desk. I folded it in half and tore it straight across. I wrote the note and glanced at my VCR clock. It was 12:08 A.M. I laid the note on the floor outside my bedroom door and flipped my light switch off before climbing out onto the roof with

Kieran. "Ready."

He laid a hand on my shoulder. A bright light flashed, and we were instantly in a park. I looked around in awe. I could see the Washington Monument all lit up, piercing the night sky.

"This is it," I said excitedly. I'm in the nation's capital! The park was well-lit, and the statues looked awesome standing high on their pedestals. "So what do we do now?" I asked, turning around to see him sitting on a park bench.

A tall, well-dressed man came along the brick walkway. Kieran stood and embraced him. "It's good to see you again, Kieran," the man said. He looked me up and down. "It's about time you gave someone eternal life," he said as he studied me. He held out a hand for me to shake, "Hi, I'm Manius."

I took his hand in mine. "I'm Kevin. It's nice to finally meet you." Kieran no doubt called him telepathically as soon as we arrived.

"Yes, he did," Manius answered my thoughts, "but I sense this little visit isn't just to introduce me to you," he added, turning his attention back to Kieran.

"Dirk has come back for me," Kieran explained. "He attempted to kill Kevin. He must be stopped before his attempts succeed."

"Attempted?" Manius questioned. He looked at me. "What was it that saved you? Let me see your thoughts." He focused his attention on me as I remembered the battle in the parking lot. After Manius saw Dirk leave from my memories, he shook his head and took a seat on the park bench to think for a moment. "It was a taunt," he finally told us. "Kieran, you must go alone if you wish to stop him."

"What?" Kieran asked, shocked by Manius' words.

"We've come here for your help," I pleaded. "We couldn't defeat—"

"I know why you've come," he cut me off, "but I cannot help you."

"You are the only person who can help," I explained. "Why won't you help us?"

"Because he's my son!" he barked.

Kieran and I stood speechless.

Manius took a deep breath before explaining. "I don't mean that he's my biological son but my immortal son. He was the first man that I gave eternal life." He looked at Kieran. "Like Kevin is your son. Could you kill your own son?"

"Never," Kieran answered without hesitation.

"The first one is always the special one," he whispered sadly. A tear of blood broke from his eye.

Kieran sat down on the bench next to him. "Well, can't you tell him to stop this?"

Manius laughed as he wiped the tear from his face. "Dirk has never been one to listen to anyone, especially his old man."

"Then what am I supposed to do?" Kieran asked him, dreading the answer he was sure to hear.

Manius thought for a moment. "Dirk didn't attempt to kill you, Kevin. He was merely demonstrating how easily he could kill you. He doesn't want you." He turned to Kieran, sitting beside him. "He wants you, and he wants you to come alone. I cannot interfere."

Kieran nodded his head and stood. "I understand," he said, knowing what he must do. "Where can

I find him?"

Manius seemed hesitant to answer. "He prefers heavily populated cities like New York, Tokyo, Mumbai, and Cairo. But Kieran," he said, standing up, "you both are very dear to me. If you can resolve this without fighting, please do." He kissed Kieran on the forehead. "Don't let hate control you."

Manius shook my hand again. "It was nice to meet you, Kevin. Let's hope next time we meet will be under better circumstances."

I said nothing but nodded in agreement.

Manius began to walk away, but in a flash, he was gone.

Kieran and I stood quietly for a moment. "I guess I need to get you home before I leave," he finally said. "Remember: If you choose to remain amongst mortals, you must appear mortal." He began to age as he spoke. "You must age, occasionally seem to be sick and, when you are ready to leave them, appear to die. You cannot attract attention to our kind." He then returned to his normal self. "I have already bestowed the power upon you, use it."

I shook my head no. "I don't want you to fight Dirk alone," I told him again. "We need a plan to take him down; not walk willingly into his trap."

"I cannot promise you that I will return," he told me, ignoring what I just said. He placed a hand on my shoulder. "I can only promise that I will do my best." He kissed me on the forehead as Manius did him. "I will do my best," he vowed.

"No," I told him. "I'm coming with you." Suddenly, I was back on the roof of my parent's house, but Kieran wasn't with me! He sent me back alone!

"NO!" I didn't have the power to teleport. All I could do was hope that he survives.

CHAPTER XVIII

THE OFFER OF IMMORTALITY

". . . And that was the last time I saw him," I said to her, finishing my story.

After sunset, Seraphine and I had moved out to a table on the terrace overlooking the Mediterranean. A couple of dimly lit lights kept the terrace from being completely dark.

Seraphine's eyes were wide with excitement. "That was a fantastic story! It was a journey through love and loss. It was a journey through friendship and loneliness. It was an . . . immortal journey," she added sadly. She took my hand and kissed my palm. She then closed my fingers over it and pushed it to my chest. "You won't have to take that journey alone," she told me.

A smile broke my sadness. "I'm glad you're here. You don't realize how special you are to me. I may not say it as often as I should but you are. I can't imagine facing eternity without you."

She blushed and slid her hand over mine. "And I can't imagine living just a single lifetime without you."

It really made me feel good to hear her say that. "Unlike Kieran, I have a chance to save the ones I love from death. I know elves live a long life of around 800 years, and you still have centuries ahead before you should worry, but you will still age over that time. Your beauty will diminish, and your health will fail. When you awaken to your last day, would your life still seem too short? Would it seem it was over in a flash?" Now I was the one placing a hand on hers. "Seraphine, if I were to offer you immortality, would you accept it?"

"I'm sorry, Kevin, but no."

I felt my heart drop. I didn't know what to say to her. I couldn't believe she said no.

She caressed my face. "I may not hold the elf belief that we fly into the Sun after death, but I still love it too much to become a vampire," she explained. "Also, I see the progress that is being made every day and the direction that technology is headed. Everyone will soon be able to live longer, healthier lives, eventually prolonging our lives indefinitely."

Amazed by this news, "I will definitely have to read up on this," I told her.

"Well, the Singularity Summit should be coming up soon," she told me with a glimmer of excitement in her eyes. "We should go."

"Yeah, I'm interested in hearing about the research being done." I thought for a moment, visualizing how the world may function if everyone were immortal. I stood and walked over to the edge of the terrace. The lights along the hillside appeared as stars. Would people need permission to have children so the world isn't overpopulated? What would happen to health insurance? What about retirement? Will people have a savings goal to reach, so they can live off the interest from then on?

"I am very grateful that you offered me immortality," she spoke up to break the silence. "And don't think that, because I turned down your offer, I plan to leave you. I love you. I wouldn't leave you to face the ages alone as Sylvia did Kieran."

I remembered Kieran telling me about the morning Sylvia left him. Even if he could go with her, he wouldn't. He wouldn't leave his sister behind. Kelena meant more to him than anything.

"Kevin?" Seraphine called me out of my thoughts.

I turned to see her on the brink of tears, and the whole world seemed threatened to collapse. She could easily take the crown as the most beautiful being in the universe. Even the Greek Goddess Aphrodite must surely be envious of her.

"You're not angry with me, are you?" Her voice reached into my very soul.

"No. Never," I answered, holding her in my arms. "I'm sorry," I apologized. "My mind was wandering."

"What were you thinking about?" she asked, her hands clasped loosely behind my neck.

I took a deep breath. "I was thinking about Kieran and the centuries that he spent alone."

"That will not be your life," she assured me.

Her words were soothing, able to lift my worries away. I nodded my head and hugged her again. We slowly pulled away and stood next to each other on the terrace overlooking the Mediterranean Ocean.

"I have another tech show to attend next week," she told me. "You're welcome to come with me, if you like."

"I think I will head home. I need to finish the book I've been writing."

Disappointedly, she said, "All right. Well how about, after the show, I catch a flight to Greensboro and come down to stay for a few days?"

"Yeah, that would be nice," I answered. "Then I can introduce you to my family."

With her eyes dry, and her smile shining brightly again, "I look forward to it." Her hand found mine, and we stood there together, facing the night sky.

ACT II

2008 AD

CHAPTER XIX

KIERAN VS DIRK

Years had passed, and I had searched the world over looking for Dirk. I couldn't give up the hunt; I would not. I would hunt him till the end of time, if I must.

I walked along the always busy streets, telepathically yelling Dirk's name. It was nearly four A.M. in the City That Never Sleeps. If I didn't find Dirk soon, I would move on to Chicago and then L.A., staying ahead of the sunrise.

"*Kieran*," Dirk's voice telepathically called out to me. "*This way*." He was leading me into Battery Park. "*Over here*," he drew my attention to him sitting alone on a park bench, looking out over the Hudson.

I took a deep breath to prepare myself as I continued walking toward him. Manius wanted me to try resolving this peacefully if possible.

"That's far enough," he said without looking at me.

I did as he said, stopping fifty feet from him. "Why have you called me out?"

"You were supposed to die ages ago on the night of Sungrove's destruction. Do you remember?" he asked, still staring out over the river.

"I did die that night," I corrected him. "I died with my family. I died with my friends. And I've walked the Earth as one of the undead every night since."

"Aww," he mocked. Dirk finally stood and turned to face me. "So touching," he said, covering his heart. "That's the problem with you elves: You love too much, and that's precisely why elves shouldn't be made into vampires," he stressed. "A vampire must be cold, ruthless, human. We take what we want and move on. You, on the other hand, actually feel sorry for them," he scolded, waving a hand toward the city. "You even go as far as helping them in their pitiful little lives," he said, sickened and confused.

"Their lives are too short to live even a single moment in despair," I justified.

"And you think taking away their pain makes facing death any easier for them? It makes no difference."

"Then why does it matter to you what I do?" I asked, my patience wearing thin.

"If it wasn't for me sending the wolves to capture you and your sister, you would have never become an immortal," he answered. "You and your sister would have been incinerated if I had sent Byron for you. Your immortality was a mistake, so I've come to correct that mistake," he told me with a maniacal grin.

"Why have you waited so long to come take it back?" I asked. "And doesn't Manius have a say in this?"

"Dear ol' dad," Dirk said with a smile. "He no longer has a say in this matter. He seems to have lost the way, so I have taken the reins."

I was suddenly confused. "I thought he had completed his quest. He has created the illusion that humans are the dominate species; they no longer believe in us."

"Illusion?" he asked. "There is no illusion," he said with a laugh. "When was the last time you saw a dragon passing as human? When was the last time you saw another elf or a fairy?"

His questions hit me like a punch in the stomach. Manius had been eliminating all of us; pitting one against the other until there was no one left but the humans. "But why has Manius let me live?" I asked him.

"He has gone soft," Dirk explained. "Not all the ancient races are extinct. I took his power to continue the quest without him. He can protect you no longer, and now I can tear the heart from your chest just as I did your sis—"

Time seemed to stand still as my hatred toward Dirk could be contained no longer, and I lunged at him, pinning him to the ground. "I will destroy you!" I yelled in his face, my voice deep and guttural.

"Your eyes . . ." he said before teleporting away from me, ". . . so much like your sisters."

I stood, taking a deep breath as my vision

returned to normal.

"There is something within you, Kieran, some hidden strength. Maybe that's why Manius has watched over you all this time. He had seen something special in you, and now I can take that power for myself." He hit his fists together side-to-side to summon an ethereal naginata, but it had a short blade on the end where it should be blunt.

"No! I won't let you!" I told him before summoning two katanas.

"I will enjoy an increase in strength," Dirk said, thirsting for power. He ran at me, spun his naginata to push my swords out of harm's way, and swept my feet out from under me. I fell hard on my back. Dirk stabbed straight down toward my chest to kill me off quickly, but I rolled out of the way, onto me feet.

We fought for a few moments, neither landing a blow.

People were coming out to start their morning jogs.

Dirk pushed both my swords to one side and made a slice along my jaw. He made an attempt to cut my head off, but I ducked under the attack and performed a leg sweep, knocking him to the ground. He quickly hopped to his feet and ran out of the park to a nearby building. He ran up the side of it to the top.

I ran to the building, but instead of running up the side, I jumped to the top. Dirk was waiting to strike, but I shielded myself with my swords. While still in the air, I put the two sword handles together to form one weapon. I flipped and landed with my weapon out behind me.

We continued to fight across building tops.

During one of Dirk's leaps to a taller building, I reached out with my right hand and telekinetically pulled him back with a quick jerk. Dirk didn't make his jump and fell. I leaped after him, holding my double blade sword with both hands over my head. Dirk grabbed hold of the side of the building to stop his fall. He saw my approaching reflection in a window, so he pushed off from the building wall to the building that he had jumped from. My weapon stabbed into the wall where he was just hanging.

Dirk and I looked at each other from across the gap. The sky was getting lighter with the approaching dawn. We leaped toward one another, meeting in air with an attack, but neither attack landed. We continued to jump back and forth from the sides of buildings, high above the city streets, but neither of us was landing a blow.

During one jump, I broke my double blade apart to, once again, make two katanas. I used one sword to block Dirk's attack and the other sword to attack. When Dirk stuck to the opposite building from me, he saw that his right forearm was badly cut. While he was distracted by the wound, I threw one of my katanas and then jumped toward him. Dirk looked just in time to see the katana pierce his shoulder. As soon as it stuck, it dissipated. Dirk lost concentration on his weapon, and it too dissipated. Dirk threw out an open hand to telekinetically stop me. I was held in midair for a moment, and then released to fall twenty-three stories. My weapon dissipated during the fall, and I landed on feet and hands. The asphalt cracked with the impact.

Dirk climbed to the top of the building to wait

for me.

I jumped fifteen stories before anyone noticed me standing in the street. I climbed the rest of the way up the building.

Dirk stood across the building from me. "You have become powerful, but you cannot defeat me," he boasted. "I have absorbed the knowledge from countless victims, making me a master of all fighting styles. Whatever secrets you have learned over the ages will soon be mine."

"How will you spend eternity if you know everything that is to be known?" I asked him.

"It is to insure my survival," he answered with a smile.

"So is that the reason why you and Manius have been eliminating us?" I asked. "Because you feel threatened?"

"You pose no real threat," Dirk answered through a laugh. "I just tire of you."

I was noticeably angered. "Like you tired of my sister? Like you tired of my home? The elves of Sungrove had never even seen a human until you came along! Because of you, I lost everyone I ever loved."

"If you had lived the life that I lived," Dirk explained, "you would understand why I've done the things I've done."

"What you have done is create madness in a world that was peaceful!" I yelled at him. All my feelings boiled to the surface.

"There is reason behind the madness," Dirk voiced.

"I fail to see it," I stated sharply.

"It isn't necessary for you to see it. My plan

only requires you to be eliminated."

I summoned an ethereal katana. "Well, let's see if you can meet those requirements."

With a wild, blood-lusting grin, Dirk ran in an arc toward me while he fired magic missiles from both hands.

I ran in an arc away from him, shielding myself from the magic missiles with my sword. I stopped and threw up my left hand to generate a force field. I threw my sword at Dirk. He summoned a katana of his own and cut through the one that I threw. Just as he cut through it, he leaped into the air and fired a bolt of lightning. It hit the ground near my feet and knocked me to the edge of the building. My head hung over the edge. I was conscious but stunned.

Dirk was dropping toward me with his sword aimed for my chest. Just before he pierced my heart, I summoned another katana and swung it to knock Dirk's sword off target. I then telekinetically pushed him away from me and jumped to my feet. Dirk's sword dissipated from the force of the push.

I ran at him with my sword. I swung down toward him, but he sidestepped it and punched me hard in the mouth, causing me to lose my sword. He followed with an uppercut. I was knocked back, and he charged into me with full force. With his hands around my arms, we both went over the edge of the building. I tried to teleport out of his grasp but couldn't. He was somehow blocking my efforts. He began laughing at me because there was nothing for me to do as we fell toward the city street below. I turned my head to see the ground approaching. His laugh became louder and deeper. Then, just before we slammed into the pavement, the sky became darker, and we were high in the air. We were still falling, but we were no longer in the city. His hands began to grow. His head became bigger. His body began to elongate, and his skin turned black as night. He soon held me with only one hand as he changed into a massive Black Dragon!

He must have learned to transform into a dragon from Manius when he fed on him in Byron's temple!

Dirk continued to laugh as we fell. I turned my head to see that we were far from human eyes. We were in the desert. I needed to free myself before I'm crushed. I tried again to teleport away, but I was unable. I summoned a sword, and it pierced through Dirk's wrist. He released me, howling in pain, and I began to free fall toward the desert floor. He folded his wings back and dove after me. He bit at me with his huge jaws, but I teleported myself to the ground below. He swooped down to catch me in his talons, but at the last second, I swung my sword, cutting a deep gash in his leg. He circled around to swoop in again, but this time, he landed hard on the sand. I saw him belch up something into his mouth. He spat, but I threw out a hand, freezing the powerful spray of acid before it could harm me. Seeing that he failed, he yelled out in anger and whipped his tail, shattering through the frozen acid. I flipped back, out of harm's way.

Dirk spread his wings and lifted himself back into the air. I shielded my eyes from the blowing sand.

"Fight me as a human, you coward!" I yelled at him, releasing my sword.

The sky began to lighten as I saw the dawn approaching again. I knew where we were now. We were in Death Valley. He teleported us ahead of the sunrise and away from people. Perhaps I could hold him here long enough so that he is destroyed by the sun. I would die too, but at least I could take him with me.

As Dirk flew toward me, I saw him shrink in size. He returned to normal just as he touched down in front of me, his wings being the last to fold away out of sight. "So be it," he said, punching me in the face.

I threw a punch at him, but Dirk deflected it with his left hand and stepped in to elbow me in the side of the face. I was getting frustrated.

Dirk threw a punch, but I caught it and threw him to the ground. I followed him down, punching all the way, but he created a force field to protect himself. I was raging, yelling louder and louder! He threw me off him, and we both slowly stood. I felt my burst of strength leave me. I must try to outsmart him if I was to win this battle.

Without blinking, we both summoned our ethereal weapons at the same time, the same weapons that we chose at the beginning of our fight. He had a naginata, and I had two katanas. We slowly circled one another.

Dirk bit his tongue and flicked blood to taunt me. I threw one of my swords and charged him. Before the sword struck him, he teleported behind me. I spun around in time to deflect a stab to my back. We fought for several moments without either of us landing an attack. Each swing made so quickly they seemed a blur. I had no time to think, only react.

I made a thrust toward his throat, but he reacted quick enough to deflect my sword up. He followed with a kick to my chin. As I pulled my sword down to defend myself from his next attack, he teleported to my side and sliced off my hand! Dirk spun and pierced my stomach with the short blade. It protruded out my back. Dirk held me up by his weapon. He got up close to me and said, with a satisfied smile, "Your blood is mine, elf." He pulled his weapon from my body, and I began to fall. He spun around and sliced in an upward arc. I hit the ground and saw my body resting on its knees. Dirk had made a diagonal cut from the left side of my stomach to under my right arm. I couldn't move, and I couldn't see Dirk. I could only see my body from that horrifying point of view.

He squatted beside me to whisper in my ear. "I have waited patiently for centuries to claim you," he said, placing a hand on my head. His hand glowed blue as he used the mind reading spell. He pulled an artery loose and began to drink, draining both my mind and my body.

I tried to scream but couldn't. I tried to block him from my thoughts, but the blood was leaving me. I was weakening. My vision grew blurry, and I lost consciousness.

I awakened! My body was smoldering. Dirk released me and backed away in confusion. What was happening to me? My body burst into flames, but it didn't hurt. It felt like my physical body was falling away to release its spirit. I rose up, looking down at my body's crumbling ashes. "I live!" I could see everything around me as if I were seeing with my entire being.

Dirk was as amazed as I was. I reached into his mind with my thoughts and saw myself through his eyes. I was light! I was fire in the form of my formal body! Wings sprouted and extended from my back!

Dirk summoned a sword and swung at me. The blade passed through me without doing any harm. He tried to teleport away, but I held him with my mind. I then grabbed him and flew high into the air.

"How can this be?" Dirk cried out. "I felt you die."

"Yes, I did die," I told him, "and I have been reborn. Now I must destroy you before your body assimilates my power."

Dirk screamed a bloodcurdling, ear-piercing scream as I absorbed him. I instantly saw his entire existence. The visions flashed so quickly that it was hard to focus, but I could feel them. There's so much hurt, so much pain, a blur of life through the ages.

I saw my sister! I followed the memories to find that he kept her heart. It was in a red plastic container held deep within an arctic facility. Many artifacts were stored there.

I took a deep breath and tried to clear my mind for a moment. I shouldn't have pulled Dirk in. There were so many memories for me to now keep separate from my own. I closed my eyes to focus on my family that died long ago. I felt my mother and father embrace me.

From fire to flesh, my new body began to change as I relaxed. My blazing wings became gold, and my skin returned to a soft white.

I opened my eyes, and my parents were with me. Was I dreaming or was I dead? "Are you here to take me to the Sun?" I asked them.

They didn't speak. They merely shook their heads.

"But I need to see," I told them. "And where is Kelena?" I asked, looking past them.

Lily and Kip kissed me on the forehead. "She will always be with you," they answered before crumbling to dust in my arms.

"Come back," I pleaded. "Please, come back." A single teardrop of liquid fire streamed down my face. I lowered my head, closed my eyes, and the teardrop fell from my face.

I felt a hand lifting my chin, and I opened my eyes. TESS! With tears streaming down my face, I closed my arms around her. We were the same height. Her wings fluttered as she too began to cry. We held each other tightly for a long moment before she pulled away and kissed me on the nose. I returned the kiss to her lips. She began to fade to light. "No," I told her, choked up from the tears. "Don't leave me. I love you."

She began to speak. "I love you too, Kieran. I have always loved you." She faded away just as the morning sun broke over the horizon.

I threw my arms up to shield my face from the sun but realized that it didn't hurt. I was not burning. I outstretched my arms and wings as I spun in the morning sun. I remembered the last sunrise before my life changed forever.

"Kieran?" I heard my sister calling.

Through tears of joy, I answered, "Yes?"

"Come on, or we'll be late," she told me once again.

Then, with more speed than I had ever imagined, I flew to the Sun. I passed through the Earth's atmosphere and zipped across space toward my destination. I could feel the roar of the Sun resonating through me as I flew closer and closer. I plunged into the immense, fiery orb and basked in its heat and the wonderful light.

The elves said the Sun was filled with the spirits of the dead, but no one was there. My family and friends must truly be dead. I may have risen victoriously from my battle with Dirk, but I felt defeated in the Sun. The stories that I heard growing up were just that. They were stories to give hope to mortals.

What should I do now? The hope of seeing my loved ones again has left me. All I have left are memories. Perhaps I should close my eyes and join them.

CHAPTER XX

A FAMILIAR VOICE

"*Kieran?*" I heard a distant voice call. "*Wake up, Kieran.*" The voice sounded familiar.

Was it within my dreams? Who called me that I could not see. The touch of a hand on my face brought me from my slumber. I opened my eyes to the brightness of the Sun and the silhouette of a woman within the light. "*Are you real, or are you from my dreams?*" I asked her. I felt her lips kiss mine.

"*I am as real as you,*" she said telepathically.

"*Sylvia! I thought you were gone forever,*" I cried, embracing her.

"*I have been waiting for you to leave your physical shell,*" she told me. "*Come outside, so I can see you more clearly.*" She took my hand, and we left the interior of the Sun. Once outside, our burning bodies appeared to solidify, taking elf form with golden wings.

"*I knew as soon as you emerged from your physical body, you would come here*," she explained.

"*Did you find the answers to your questions?*" I asked, remembering she left to find the one who made her over a millennium ago.

"*I did*," she answered with a smile. "*Ambros found me here just as I have you. He too had grown up hearing that, after death, the spirit flies into the Sun. Once he found me, we visited each of the planets and moons in this system before we ventured farther out into the galaxy. When I felt your body die, I came here to look for you.*"

"*Where is Ambros now?*" I asked.

"*He continued on until I can meet back up with him. He told me that we are a special race of vampires that evolve by assimilating knowledge and power to grow past the flesh. Ambros achieved this by drinking the blood of a phoenix. The phoenix had found him to be of an interesting species, and let itself be known to him the only way a vampire could know it—through the drinking of its blood.*"

"*So Ambros absorbed the power to transcend death and has passed that power onto his descendants*," I reiterated.

"*Yes*," she confirmed. Her expression turned sad, and I knew what she was about to ask. "*So how did Serena die?*"

Unable to tell her, I shook my head and tears filled our eyes. She pulled me close, and we held each other for a long moment. Remembering how we used to spin in the air, I began to do it once again. Our tears fell away, and our sadness turned to smiles.

"*Oh, how I've missed you,*" she said, running her fingers through my hair.

"*I've missed you too.*"

She flew back a few feet and extended a hand to me. "*So are you ready to explore the galaxy?*"

Knowing that she was not going to like my answer, I pressed my lips together and shook my head.

"*You have given someone eternal life. You have an immortal son, don't you?*"

"*Am I that transparent?*" I laughed. "*I'm sorry, but I can't leave yet. There is someone that I need to see first.*"

She nodded her head in acceptance. "*When will you be ready?*"

I stared off into space toward a distant Earth. "*I don't know,*" I answered.

She turned my face to hers. "*Don't be gone too long,*" she repeated with a smile. I had said the same to her ages ago.

I drew her into my arms. "*I won't be.*" I began to slowly pull away from her. Neither of us seemed sad this time. We were happy to see each other again. As soon as our hands broke free from one another's, I flew away from her.

Streaking through the blackness of space, I sped toward Earth. I pierced the atmosphere that surrounded our planet and flew across a magnificent, blue ocean to arrive in the Arctic Circle. I touched down on a frozen mountain where a large, steel entrance protruded from the ice. I knew that it must be dreadfully cold there, but it didn't affect me.

I walked up to the locked door and passed through it as if it were made of water. Inside, I found a long corridor cut deep into the mountain. The lights were off, but I didn't need them. I walked to the end of the corridor and left through a series of airlocks. I entered a large room filled with shelves. I followed Dirk's memories to a large, red plastic container placed among others on a shelf with a barcode and a series of numbers printed on it. "This is it," I told myself, picking up the container. I unscrewed the lid to make sure there really was a heart within it, and there was. It was frozen in blood. I looked around the room at all the plastic storage containers. I wanted to look through them all, but now wasn't the time; I needed to get Kel's heart thawed. I closed my eyes and vanished.

END

ACT II

CHAPTER XXI

SHE WANTS BLOOD

It was just after midday, and I was sitting in the shade at my home in Seagrove. I was finally finishing up my book. It's nonfiction, but of course, it will be released as fiction. It's forbidden for me to prove that vampires exist and besides, this story is too fantastic to believe anyway.

Suddenly, Kieran appeared in the yard! The sun didn't seem to harm him! He looked over the house and casually stepped up on the porch.

"What took you so long?" I jokingly asked, playing off my excitement. I stood to greet him.

"Sorry," he answered, glancing at my shaved head. "I must have dozed off."

We hugged each other.

"I was reborn," he went on to tell me, "reborn from the ashes of my own body." He glanced again at my head.

"Would you like to sit?" I asked him, motioning to another chair at the wrought iron table. "I'm sure you have plenty to tell."

"I do have much to tell you, but first, I need your help."

"Of course," I agreed, wondering how I could possibly help someone as powerful as Kieran.

"We should go before it gets cold," he told me.

Being late summer, I was confused by this, but I didn't ask questions. I shut down my computer and took it inside. I grabbed my hoodie and rejoined Kieran on the porch, locking the door behind me.

"You won't need the hoodie," he told me. "We won't be in the sun."

Becoming more confused, I threw it over the back of a chair.

"You haven't aged a bit," he pointed out. "You've only shaved your head to change your appearance."

"I want to stay young," I explained.

Unable to resist any longer, he rubbed my head. "For luck," he said with a laugh. He then took hold of my wrist. A white light enveloped us, and when the light extinguished, we were in a large, round room surrounded by statues. This was Kieran's home, hidden away in the Virginia Mountains. The ceiling was supported by marble columns. Orbs of light were positioned around the wall and on the columns. In the center of the room, resting on a pedestal, was the statue of him, his sister, and Tess. I stepped forward to get a closer look at the statue that I had heard him speak of so many times before and noticed that the pool was filled with blood.

"Where did all this blood come from?" I asked.

"It's animal blood," he answered, walking past me. Just when it looked like he would step into the pool, he began to float across to the statue. He caressed Kelena's face, and his eyes began to glow red with the fiery tears that filled them.

"Hi Kel. I'm sorry I've been gone for so long, but I come to you now with the power to bring you back." He put his arms around her. The marble statue of Kelena began to liquefy and melt like mud, slowly running down the column into the pool. There was a body encased within it! Her body! He carefully lifted her from the pedestal. Without getting his feet wet, he carried her to the edge of the pool.

He extended a hand to a red plastic jar on a table, and it came to him. "Hold onto this for a moment," he told me.

I took the container and looked down into it to examine its contents. It was full of blood.

Kieran ran his finger from her bellybutton to her neck, and her skin was cut with an invisible force. He then broke open her rib cage.

I winced and looked away for a moment. To be a vampire, I'm awfully squeamish, especially when it comes to opening chest cavities. Ugh.

"All right, give me the heart, Kevin," he ordered.

"The heart?" I asked, looking at the jar in disgust. "There's a heart in here?"

Kieran held a hand out for me to give him the heart. I slowly poured the blood out over my hand and caught the heart that slid out. I was a bit grossed out by it as I placed it in Kieran's waiting hand.

I watched him put the heart in its rightful place, lining up arteries as best he could. "Now," he said, looking up at me, "I need your blood to bring her back."

"My blood?" I questioned.

"Yes, my body no longer circulates the blood that she needs," he explained. "She won't need all of it," he added with a smile; "only enough to heal her heart and get it pumping again."

With a nod, I agreed and knew what I must do. I sliced my wrist with a small, ethereal knife. The blood ran down my hand and from my fingers onto Kelena's heart.

Kieran lifted one of the heart's broken arteries. "Let some of it run inside."

Starting to feel weak, I sat down at the edge of the pool and let my blood run into the heart. My wrist tried to heal, but I kept the wound pulled open.

Kieran lined up the artery, and I continued to saturate the area. He closed the chest and told me "That's enough."

I pulled my hand back and held the wound shut so that I could heal faster. I was still very weak and would need to feed soon.

Kieran stepped into the waist-deep pool and scooped his sister up in his arms. He lowered her into the blood, leaving only her face visible. "Please work," he wished aloud. "Come on, wake up. Wake up, Kel. Please wake up," his words became whispers.

I sat back against a marble column and examined my wrist to see that it had nearly healed. I looked around the room at all the statues. He must have spent a lot of time on each because they were highly detailed. There were also framed drawings hanging on the walls, most of them having only a small amount of color.

A gasp brought my attention back to Kieran, but it wasn't him. It was Kelena! She drew breath!

"Kevin," Kieran called for me. "Get out of here!" He struggled to hold her without doing any harm, while she writhed and gnashed her teeth.

"The sun is still out," I reminded him.

"There are plenty of trees to keep the sun off you," he informed me. "Just get out of here. She is changing, and she wants blood!"

"Well, dip her," I told him, motioning with my hands for him to submerge her.

"She smells you. She wants your blood," he specified, trying to hold her. "Hurry!"

I made my way across the room and up the stairs to a large, metal door. I tried to open it, but it wouldn't budge. I heard Kieran struggling more and more. I pushed with all my strength but couldn't open the door. "Kieran, I'm too weak. I can't get out!" I turned around, and there was a blood-soaked werewolf, on all fours, looking up at me from the bottom of the stairs. Not even a gasp escaped me as my entire body began shaking.

The wolf leaped up the stairs after me, but in an instant, Kieran was there! The werewolf slammed into a force field that Kieran had erected. The beast fell down the steps but charged back up after me. It took chunks of stone out of the wall as it tried to dig around the force field.

"It appears that we are in a tight spot," I joked,

feeling better now that Kieran stood between me and the bloodthirsty monster.

"Yes, it appears so," Kieran agreed, catching my sarcasm. "We can't teleport out and expect Kel to stay down here forever."

"She is no longer Kelena. She is a monster," I told him as the beast continued to claw away stone.

"She has no memories," he corrected me. "There is only the animal in her, and it needs to feed. I tried to give her back memories of our childhood, but she attacked me. I couldn't concentrate on transferring memories and hold her still at the same time."

"If she wants me, then let her have me," I told him in a dreadful tone.

Still holding the force field with both hands, he turned his head quickly to look at me. "What? No! She will kill you!"

"You arose from your death," I reminded him. "I believe I will from mine, and while she is feeding on me, you can give her memories back."

Knowing what must be done, he nodded his head. He turned his attention back to his feral sister as she dug around our invisible shield and clawed for me. "I'm sorry," Kieran said. He then lowered the force field and charged into Kelena! In a blur of motion, he sped down the stairs, carrying his sister away from me. Howling, the wolf tried to break free from his grasp but couldn't.

I hurried down the stairs in time to see them slam into what was left of the center statue. Along with the broken marble, they disappeared into the pool.

"Kieran! Kieran!" I yelled, but the pool went calm. I stood there, unsure of what I should do, but then the blood in the pool began to bubble and boil.

Kieran stood within the pool. He rose to the top and walked across the boiling blood. It didn't stain him. It evaporated to leave him perfectly clean. As he stepped from the pool, it stopped boiling and went calm again. His face looked as cold as stone.

"Why didn't you let me hold her attention?" I asked on the verge of tears.

"Because I won't put your life in danger!" he yelled, grabbing me by the shoulders. "Your body is your only real possession. I won't let you throw it away so easily."

The pool exploded, and out of the blood, a woman of fire spread her wings! She looked directly at us and breathed in deeply, her fire burning hot. She flew toward us, her body appearing to cool and become flesh. Her bare feet touched the cold, stone floor, and clothing began to grow up her slender, elven frame. With her thick, strawberry blonde curls, emerald eyes, and finely crafted features, Kelena was simply . . . beautiful.

Tears of liquid fire streamed down Kieran's face, and he fell to his knees; his legs no longer able to hold him up in the presence of his sister.

And then she spoke. "Kieran?"

EPILOGUE

With all that I've seen and all that Kieran has told me so far, it seems I've written quite a book. I can only imagine what else he has witnessed throughout his long life. Speaking of Kieran, he should be back soon. He took his sister on a quick tour of the world, but he told me that, when they return, we will take another trip to D.C. to have a word with Manius. As for me, I'm at home enjoying the day as any vampire would—in the shade.

THE IMMORTAL EPIC

WILL CONTINUE WITH

IMMORTAL CONQUEST